MY MOM'S ⊿   ⌐H

Debbie Aubrey

ISBN-13: 9798721390708
ISBN-10: 1477123456

May 2022
Cover design by: Art Painter
Library of Congress Control Number: 2018675309
Printed in the United States of America

For John, Barry and Robert x

CHAPTER ONE

Mom had changed her face again. I never knew what she was going to look like from one day to the next. It was really annoying.

Yesterday she'd been Lady Gaga, but Mom had got the proportions all wrong and Lady Gaga's tiny head wobbled like a ping-pong ball on top of Mom's tall, slim body. I said to her, "Mom, you look too stupid for words," and she told me off for being cheeky. It wasn't easy keeping a straight face when her voice sounded like Mickey Mouse sucking helium.

This morning I encountered a really old woman at the breakfast table. Even Merlina, our cat, who was silently sitting in the sugar bowl on the table, seemed startled by the horrendous sight.

"This isn't right," Mom grumbled, staring at her grey wrinkled skin and sparse grey hair in a hand mirror. "I wanted to look like Bette Davies when she was young and gorgeous, not dead and decomposed like this."

I tutted and shoved a spoonful of cornflakes into my mouth so I wouldn't have to comment. Mom *always* asks me what I think of her different appearances. She gets upset it I admit that I just want her to look like my Mom.

I wouldn't mind so much if she kept the same face for a few weeks, even a few months, so I'd have time to get used to it. I might even be able to recognise my own mother in the streets.

As it is, I often have to walk up to someone I *think* is my mother, and ask, "Excuse me, are you Mom?" Sometimes I get it wrong and complete strangers look at me as if I've completely flipped my lid. It's very embarrassing.

Mom stared at her reflection in the mirror, huffing and grumbling a lot. Then she put the mirror down by her bowl of pickled spinach. That's another thing about my Mom. Not only does she look different every morning, she also likes pickles for breakfast. Pickles with gripe-water! She says it gives her spirits a boost.

"It's no good," Mom said. "I'll have to change it again."

"Oh Mom!" I groaned. "What's wrong with you *own* face? It's pretty - "

"Pretty boring," she said. "I've had it for over two hundred years, Crystal. I like to have a new face every now and again."

"But you do it two or three times *a day*," I complained.

"So?"

"So, isn't that a complete waste of magic power?"

Mom looked at me with her dry, protruding eyeballs and baggy mouth. "It's *my* magic," she said, "I can do whatever I like with it."

I gave up. It was useless to argue with Mom. The Chief Magician had already warned her to cut down on spells before her magic supply collapsed with exhaustion, but she kept on doing it.

Mom opened a magazine and quickly flicked through the pages. I knew what she was doing, she was looking for a suitable photograph of a famous model or film star to copy.

"What about Kate Middleton, the princess?" she asked. "She's a warm, funny, intelligent woman. It might be nice to be intelligent for a while."

"You'd just have the looks, Mom, not the brain cells," I sighed. "It would take more than a face change to make you intelligent.

"Don't be so cheeky, young lady. I have lots of certificates and diplomas - "

"They're all *fake*, Mom."

Mom tutted. I sighed.

Apart from changing her face every ten minutes or so, Mom's other favourite habit is collecting awards. Whenever she hears on the news or reads in the newspaper about someone winning a prize, she gets jealous and conjures up the same award with her name on it.

There are boxes of them in the attic, along with medals and trophies, and even rosettes from horse shows. None of them are real. Mom just likes to show them off occasionally. I don't know what people must think when she puts fifteen Oscars on the living room windowledge for all the world to admire. She's never even watched a film, let alone starred in one.

I *do* know that our neighbours all think she's brilliant. They see all these trophies and awards in the window and assume she's some kind of genius. Little do they know that my mother has the memory of a goldfish and is totally incapable of performing the simplest spell without getting it wrong.

I'll never forget the day I came home from school and Mom flew into a wild panic because my tea wasn't ready. I didn't mind, but Mom was convinced I'd starve to death if I didn't have it right there and then.

She sprinted into the kitchen and told the cooker to prepare a cheese salad. A salad from the cooker, I ask you! Everyone knows that it's the *fridge* that makes salads.

Anyway, what she got out of the oven defies any sort of description. It was all black and crispy and looked more like a compost heap than a meal. Even Cuthbert, our hairy mongrel dog, wouldn't touch it when I offered him some.

And then there was the time Mom decided our house was looking a little dull and decided to redecorate. Not just one room at a time, like normal people, but the whole house all in one go. She overloaded her magic and her spellcasting went haywire.

We had a bright orange living room, complete with bright orange furniture, dark purple bedrooms, and luminous green moss growing on the kitchen walls. Mom attempted to reverse it all and change it back, but she got her spells wrong again and everything turned as black as night - even the lightbulbs!

In desperation, she blasted a handful of magic into the air and turned the entire house into pink cardboard. The walls buckled and the roof sagged.

We eventually got our brick walls back, but we now live in a crooked, multi-coloured house which looks like a battered birthday present. The wallpaper gives me headaches.

Mom interrupted my thoughts by making my breakfast bowl disappear before I'd even finished my cornflakes.

"Crystal," she said, in the kind of voice that meant she wanted me to agree with her about something, "What do you think of Marge Simpson?"

I told her there was no way I was having a cartoon character for a mother. She pulled a face, which wasn't easy with Bette Davies' dead face.

By the time I left for school that morning, Mom was floating down the hallway in a really tight designer outfit trying to be Angelina Jolie. Unfortunately, she hadn't concentrated hard enough and was actually wearing the face of a character out of Coronation Street instead. I hadn't the heart to tell her.

It was raining outside. The dark sky promised thunderstorms and real bucketing weather. I stood on the doorstep and sighed.

I no longer owned a raincoat. Not one that fitted, anyway. Mom had shrunk it down to toddler size in her one attempt to work the washing machine 'manually'. I didn't have an umbrella either, Merlina had used it to sharpen her claws so it now looked like a Hawaiian grass skirt.

The rain pelted down. I was going to get soaked. Unless ... ?

It wasn't allowed but, after checking no one was around to see, I magicked up a brand new umbrella - one of those massive ones they use to walk around golf courses.

I stepped into the downpour, dry and well-pleased with myself. Unlike Mom, I usually get my spells right.

A few doors down the road I stopped to call for Dayle. Dayle is my best friend and we always walk to school together. I like her because she's normal, she has normal parents and lives in a normal house.

It wasn't until I met Dayle and started going to ordinary

school that I realised how strange and unusual my parents were. Before that I'd attended The School for Spellmakers, which had goblins and elves and fairies for pupils. The lessons were easy. We learned how to make magic and never did any boring stuff like Maths and English. It was fun.

Then Mom decided I wasn't getting a 'proper education' and wasn't mixing with the 'right sort of people', so we left our Welsh cave in the Black Mountains and moved into a council house on a big estate in Birmingham. It was a bit awkward at first because a family were already living in the house at the time, but Mom gave them a big suitcase full of money and they went away quite happily.

I remember my very first day at the local comprehensive school. Miss Evans, my form teacher, made me stand up in front of the whole class to introduce me to everyone. She asked what my hobbies were, if I had any pets, what job my father did for a living.

"Oh, my Dad's not living," I said. "He's dead."

Miss Evans face went as white as a ghost, which seemed appropriate. "I'm *so* sorry, Crystal," she said, "I didn't know."

The entire class made sad noises, like the mooing of cows.

"But he visits us quite often," I added.

The class fell silent. Miss Evans looked embarrassed, then confused, then annoyed. It wasn't until later I discovered that other children didn't have ghosts for fathers. Nor did they have witch mothers who made things appear out of thin air, who told stories with ghostly pictures floating around the room, or who slept on the ceiling at night. Other children's parents didn't seem to do anything interesting at all.

Dayle rolled miserably out of her house with her head hanging down. Without saying a word, she dragged her feet along the pavement, splashing her shoes in the puddles and not looking at all bothered by the waterfall of rain cascading down on her head. She refused to share my bright new umbrella.

"What's up?" I asked.

Dayle thrust her hands into her soggy blazer pockets and mumbled, "I've got Biology this morning."

5

"I thought you liked Biology?"

"I do, but I've got Haig Mullins sitting next to me this term."

"He's not still picking on you, is he?"

Dayle nodded her dripping head, her long hair hanging like wet curtains on either side of her face, and sniffed.

Haig Mullins is the school bully. He picks on anyone who dares cross his path, and looks like one of those pictures you see of stone age man, all sloping forehead and long arms. He acts like one, too.

Last term he'd made Dayle's life a misery, pinching her books, tripping her up in the corridor and taking her dinner tickets off her until she almost starved to death. The teachers didn't do much to help, they're all scared of him too.

I guess that was why Dayle was so determined to walk in the rain all the way to school. She obviously wanted to catch a cold or flu or some other damp-related disease so she wouldn't have to go to school and face Haig for a while.

I attempted to cheer her up by telling her what my mother had done over the weekend. Dayle knows my Mom is a witch, it's our little secret. But she didn't crack a smile when I told her Mom had argued with the cat about a missing tin of pilchards, and had turned Cuthbert into a jellyfish just to see if he would like it.

The closer we got to school the more depressed Dayle became. By the time we stood outside our form class waiting for our teacher to arrive, she was almost in tears. Haig glared at her from the other side of the corridor.

"You got my money, pale whale?" he grunted.

Dayle glowed like a red light bulb and tried to look invisible.

"Why don't you leave her alone?" I snapped. "And stop threatening to hurt people if they don't give you money, it's called blackmail and it's against the law."

Haig grinned. It wasn't a nice grin, his teeth were all crooked. "Why don't you mind you own business, *Glassy*," he spat.

"My name is *Crystal*," I spat back. "You only call people nasty names because your tiny little brain can't remember their real ones."

The grin dropped from Haig's face like a rock. He stepped forward across the corridor, his eyes squinting, his mouth making a zigzag pattern across his chin. I almost screamed and ran off, but my feet felt like they were glued to the floor and I couldn't move.

Instead, I pretended I was brave. Inside, a little coward started screaming for help.

"You saying I'm stupid or summat?" Haig demanded to know.

My mouth opened of its own accord and started talking without my permission. "Just don't leave your brain to medical science," the mouth said, "Unless they have a good microscope to see it with."

Half the class burst out laughing, the other half sucked in air and shuffled to the furthest end of the corridor. My entire life flashed before my eyes. It didn't take long.

Haig frowned. He clenched his fists and made a noise like he was a human bomb about to explode. His eyes peered at me from beneath his sloping forehead, and then...

...Miss Evans arrived. Oh thank goodness! My heart stopped struggling to get out of my chest and I heaved a huge sigh of relief.

As I darted through the door into the classroom, Haig grabbed hold of my hair and snarled, "I'll get you later, Glassy."

All my internal organs wrapped themselves around my soft, yellow backbone.

We sat down at our desks. Dayle lifted the lid of hers and put her head inside, trying to pull the lid down and disappear. "You shouldn't have said anything to him," she whimpered, "You've made it worse. Now he'll never leave me alone."

"No need to thank me for sticking up for you!" I said. "I'm always willing to help a friend in need."

Dayle was silent all through registration and didn't emerge from inside her desk until the bell rang for first lesson. Biology. She shuffled miserably out of the form class like a woman condemned.

It wasn't a very good morning for me, either. I had two periods of English with a teacher who was madly in love with

7

Shakespeare. She kept rattling on and on about how much Romeo loved Juliet, and didn't seem to notice that several people were slumped in a deep sleep across their desks.

At breaktime I met Dayle in the girl's toilets. She was still in a bad mood.

"Haig prodded and punched me all through the lesson," she said. "I told Mr Wallis and he moved Haig to another desk, but then Haig kept flicking locusts at me. He said if I don't pay him fifty pence by tomorrow he's going to get me, and it's all your fault, Crystal."

"Why don't you tell him to get lost?"

Dayle huffed loudly and put her hands on her non-existent hips. "Because I like living, that's why," she said. "It's easy for *you* to give advice. *You're* not the one he's got it in for, are you."

"Only because I stand up to him," I said.

"*That's* only because you're too afraid to move," she said.

Sometimes it's not good to have a friend who knows me so well.

We stood in silence for a while, in the girl's toilet, picking at a swollen toilet roll in the sink. Then Dayle turned to me and smiled this really gooey smile.

"Could you do me an enormous favour, Crystal?"

"I can't," I said, shaking my head, "You know I can't."

"Please, Crystal, old pal," she begged. "Just one tiny, itsy-bitsy spell to make Haig leave me alone. Turn him into something harmless, like a frog or a bowl of custard."

"I'm not allowed, Dayle. I'm not supposed to perform magic spells on my own yet. My Mom would go mad if she found out - "

"She won't know, will she? Oh, go on, Crystal. *Please.*"

I felt my face twitching. It would be so easy to do, and Mom wouldn't find out unless she inspected her magic bank account, which she hardly ever did.

But then, if I did one favour for Dayle she'd be pestering me for more until the end of time.

Last week she'd wanted me to make her favourite boy band appear in her bedroom. The week before that she'd wanted a stretched limousine to chauffeur her to school when she was feeling particularly lazy.

"I'm sorry," I said. "I can't do it."

Dayle stormed out of the girl's toilets yelling, "Some friend you are!"

I felt terrible.

To complete an already grotty morning, I had History. Normally I like History, we were doing medieval times with all those castles and great feats of bravery.

But that morning Mr Fripps, our History teacher, decided to do a lesson about medieval witches. My stomach did a double back-flip as soon as he said it.

"Ignorant people in those days believed in witches and curses," he began, "If a farmer had a bad crop or a child suddenly fell ill, the whole village would march up to the nearest old-age pensioner and accuse her of being a witch."

It was all a bit too close to home.

"There were two methods of dealing with witches," Mr Fripps continued. "One was to tie them up and throw them into deep water. If they drowned, they were innocent, but if they floated it was proof that they possessed evil powers. Seems a little unfair to me."

The class laughed. I felt all my internal organs slide down to my feet like blancmange. Grandma had once been thrown into a river when she was young. She'd turned herself into a fish - a salmon, I think - and had swum six miles upstream in order to escape. Grandma had hated water and fish - particularly salmon - ever since.

Mr Fripps opened a book and showed everyone a full-colour picture. "This was another method of dealing with witches," he said. "They burned them at the stake."

I fell off my chair and crawled out of the classroom on my hands and knees. Mr Fripps followed and ordered me back into class. When I refused to return he made me write out three hundred lines of *I must not cower in the corridor during History lesson.*

The day dragged on. At lunch time I ate what the canteen laughingly called food and tried to get Dayle to speak to me. She only sat at my table so she could practice her dirty looks. Her dirty looks made her look silly. I didn't help matters by telling her she looked silly.

In the afternoon I fought with chronic indigestion and had my brain pulverised by the new Maths teacher. He asked me what a square root was. I told him it was a freak of nature as vegetables were never square. He called me an imbecile. I looked it up in the dictionary later. I don't think I made a very good impression on him.

Finally, the home time bell rang out and two thousand children poured down the school driveway in a tidal wave of bag-swinging noise. I saw Dayle being attacked at the gates - not by Haig Mullins but by a first year wanting a kiss. This first year has an enormous crush on Dayle and follows her around like an adoring puppy begging for attention. Dayle thinks he's "uber gross".

Anyway, this little kid was bouncing up and down in front of her with his lips puckered and Dayle was making retching sounds and pushing him away. It looked so funny, I laughed.

Big mistake, *huge* mistake. If there's anything Dayle hates more than being told she looks silly it's being laughed at. She grappled the first year to the ground, snarled at me, and stormed off in a huff - for the second time that day! I had to walk home alone.

Feeling miserable, I took a detour across the park. I like the park. It's full of birds and dogs and children trying to kill themselves in the playground.

My friends live there too. I found them pecking for worms on the football pitch.

CHAPTER TWO

"Hi, Maggie," I called out. "Hi, B.W."

They squawked at me loudly and flapped their black and white wings in welcome. Maggie flew up onto my shoulder.

"Hello, caw-Crystal," she screeched, in that dry, crusty voice of hers. "Don't bother talking to B.W., he's in one of his moods again."

"Oh dear," I said. "You two haven't been arguing again, have you?"

"There's not much else to do around here except argue, and B.W is *so* moody he takes offence over every little thing."

"I do not!" he croaked.

Maggie shoved her beak into my ear. It tickled. "He's upset because I found a shiny silver bottle top yesterday and all he found was a rusty old nail. I told him to throw it away because it's heavy and keeps falling through the nest, but he insists on keeping it."

I shook my head. Maggie and B.W were *always* fighting about who found the best trinkets. I don't think the trinkets mattered, really, I think they just like an excuse to fight with each other.

Maggie flew down and landed right next to B.W., piercing him with a nasty glare from her beady black eyes. B.W. ignored her and turned his back for a good sulk but, feeling nervous with Maggie behind him, he kept twitching his head from side to side to make sure she didn't start tugging at his tail feathers.

"So, what have you been up to today?" I asked.

For a split second they both stared blankly into space. "Caw, what *have* we done today?" B.W. forced himself to ask Maggie.

"Same as yesterday, I guess," she replied.

"And what did we do yesterday?"

"The same as we did today."

"Forget it," I said.

I sat at a wooden picnic table and watched them for a while. They were funny birds. I knew they loved each other a lot but they pretended not to. Maybe all Magpies are like that.

Maggie screamed at B.W. B.W. screamed back. They sounded like a couple of old car engines trying to start up on a cold morning. Maggie pecked B.W. for screaming so loud, and B.W. took offence and flew off to sulk underneath a tree. Then he spotted the head of a worm sneaking out of the ground. Maggie immediately rushed over with her wings flapping, claiming that she saw it first. Their beaks clashed as they fought over the worm, while the worm looked up at them in amazement.

They flew up into the branches of the tree, shrieking and spluttering at each other. The worm turned to me, bunched his slimy body up into a shrug, then returned to the ground. Maggie noticed the now absent worm and blamed B.W., chasing him from the top of one tree to another, weaving and plummeting between them like invisible stitches.

I waited for a while but they didn't come back, so I went home.

Mom wasn't in the house when I got in, which was unusual. I asked Cuthbert where she'd gone.

"To see your Dad," he growled, watching Merlina tearing his blanket to pieces with her claws.

"What has she gone to see Dad for?"

"Apparently," Cuthbert said, "He's been refused permission to visit us again, so your mother has gone to sort it out."

I didn't like the sound of that. I sighed and flopped into an armchair - a blotchy, multi-coloured armchair by the blotchy multi-coloured fireplace.

The last time Mom had gone to 'sort things out' she'd caused havoc in the Spectre Department. They tried to throw her out of the Ghost Bureau, but she dragged all the supervisors' heads home in her handbag. For three days our living room had been filled with all sorts of ghostly apparitions and spooky spectres, all arguing that Dad should spend more time haunting, and could the supervisors have their heads back please.

Dad is *supposed* to haunt full time, but he keeps making excuses to come home and stay with us instead. Dad doesn't like scaring people very much, and he gets lonely stuck in stately homes and castle ruins all on his own.

"I don't suppose Mom made me anything to eat before she left, did she?" I asked.

Cuthbert head-butted Merlina out of his bed and possessively plonked his hairy body down on his now tattered blanket. "There's something in the oven," he barked, as Merlina sauntered up the banister rail with her tail and her nose held high, "But don't ask me what it's supposed to be."

I went to take a look. I couldn't identify the bubbling green goo in a casserole dish either, and the oven just made retching noises like it was about to be sick when I asked what it was, so I made myself some toast instead.

Cuthbert, certain that his precious bed was safe from invasion for a while, padded into the kitchen.

"That cat has been driving me mad all day," he said. "If she's not sticking her nails into my nose, she's deliberately destroying my plastic toys. Do you know what she did this morning?" he whined. I shook my head. "She climbed up a tree with my favourite bone and dared me to go up and get it. I nearly broke my neck."

"Dogs aren't supposed to climb trees, Cuthbert."

"I know that *now*."

He sauntered over to his bowl and sniffed inside, not really expecting to find anything but checking just in case.

"Have you been fed?" I asked.

"Not since last Thursday."

"Don't exaggerate, Cuthbert. I'm sure Mom wouldn't starve you on purpose."

"She doesn't do it on purpose." He collapsed onto the rug - the blotchy, multi-coloured carpet by the blotchy, multi-coloured sink. "She forgets, or she thinks she's already fed me. I had to make my own breakfast this morning."

"Poor Cuthbert. What did you have?"

"Bacon and eggs. At least the cooker knows how to look after an old dog."

A tiny voice from the corner of the kitchen squeaked, "Any time, Cuthbert".

I gave his furry body a big hug.

Mom came home quite late that night. She breezed into the living room like a sparkling tornado and immediately turned on the television.

"Oh poo!" she cried, "I've missed The Real Housewives, and I wanted to get a good look at that new woman with the big lips and enormous chest."

"You're not going to change your face *again* are you, Mom?" I groaned.

Mom turned round to look at me. It was then that I noticed she was wearing her own face. It's a nice face, with large green eyes, long black hair, and a pouting red mouth. I don't know why she doesn't like it, why she keeps trying to make herself look better by borrowing other people's faces. I think she's beautiful.

Except when she's angry. And she looked angry now. Her eyes were so wide I thought they might pop out of her head, and her voice echoed around the living room like the rumbling of thunder.

"What's wrong with changing my face?" she roared at me.

I was shocked. Mom never gets angry and *never* raises her voice at me, unless...

"What happened with Dad today?" I asked.

Mom's anger vanished in a puff of smoke, literally a puff of smoke. She sat down next to me on the multi-coloured sofa and wrapped an arm around my shoulders. "They've put him on overtime," she sighed. "They say he has to make up his haunting hours or he'll be transferred to the Lost Souls Department."

"But Dad isn't a lost soul," I cried, "He belongs here, with us."

"They say he doesn't belong to us any more because he's dead."

"That's silly! He's my Dad!"

"I know, Crystal. I know."

Mom hugged me. I wanted to cry, but I didn't in case it made Mom cry, too.

"Where's Dad now?" I asked, blinking back tears.

"He's in some deserted castle in Scotland, waiting to scare the living daylights out of some passing tourists. He has to stay there for six months."

"Six months!"

"Your father and I aren't happy about it either, Crystal."

"But isn't there anything we can do? You've helped him escape his haunts before?"

"Not this time." Mom sighed. She frowned and bit her bottom lip. I could tell she was trying not to cry. "They said if I make him desert his post or kidnap him again they'll send him to another country where we'll never be able to find him. And you know how much he hates going abroad and having to mix with all those foreign ghosts."

I hugged her tightly. "We'll think of something, Mom. I'm sure it'll be alright."

When I came down to breakfast the next morning, Mr Andrews from next door was sitting at the kitchen table talking to Mom.

" - and when I woke up this morning," he was saying, his eyes wide in astonishment, "They were *10 times* the size!"

Mom's mouth twitched into a satisfied smirk. She'd been up to her old tricks again, I could tell.

The trouble with my Mom is she's too soft-hearted. She'll do anything for anyone, whether it's against the rules or not. When Mrs Jones from down the road complained about her very shouty neighbours, Mom gave them all a severe dose of tonsillitis, which kept them quiet for weeks.

And when Mr Smith a few doors away casually mentioned that he'd like a dog as a companion but wasn't able to make it to the nearest dogs home to choose one, Mom transported an assortment of animals from the dogs home into his back garden to pick from. He actually kept them all.

And whenever Mom hears on the news about some catastrophe in another country, or a charity desperately needing funds, she withdraws cash from millionaires' bank accounts and donates it in their name. None of the millionaires ever complain, Mom says it's good publicity for them.

Now she'd heard about Mr Andrews being keen to enter the amateur garden festival with his pumpkins. He usually grew whoppers, but this year the weather had been bad. Last night they had been the size of tomatoes. This morning they were as big as beach balls.

I gave Mom a look as I poured cornflakes into my breakfast bowl, but she continued to look innocent as Mr Andrews ranted and raved about his spectacular vegetables. He was a very happy man.

Which is more than could be said for Dayle when I went to call for her. She still had a face like a sour lemon, and it was all I could do to get her to talk.

"Cuthbert and Merlina had another big bust-up last night," I said, watching her face for any spark of interest. "He said she was a flea-bitten rat-catcher, and she called him a dirty, smelly hairball. They chased each other around the house all night and I couldn't get to sleep." Nothing from Dayle. "And Mom was banging her head on the ceiling all night, too."

I thought I detected some slight movement on Dayle's face, as if she considered smiling but couldn't be bothered. So I pounded her on the back and yelled, "What's the matter, mate?"

She looked at me then. There was a mixture of fury and misery in her blue eyes. "What do you think is the matter, Crystal?"

"Haig Mullins, right?"

"Right. Mom wouldn't let me have my pocket money early

this week. If I don't give him fifty pence today he's going to do terrible things to me."

"Ignore him," I said.

"Hard to ignore someone who is trying to strangle you with your own hair."

Dayle didn't speak again for a while and we continued to walk to school in silence. Then she said, "Crystal," and I knew from the tone of her voice that she was after something again.

"No," I said.

"I haven't asked you anything yet."

"I know what you want and the answer is no."

"*Please*, Crystal, I'm *begging* you! Can't you do something about him? Send him to Siberia or, better still, the moon."

"Dayle, I'd love to help you, I really would - "

"But you can't." She rolled her eyes and tutted. "Forget I asked."

Haig was onto her the minute she stepped into the playground. He stomped across the tarmac like an upright hippopotamus, scattering pupils all over the place, and barged into her with his broad shoulder. Dayle almost fell over.

"Where's my money, Pale Whale?" he demanded. "I want my money."

"I haven't got it," she whimpered. "Please go away and leave me alone."

A few kids gathered around to watch, all of them relieved they weren't the one Haig was picking on.

"If I don't get my money *today*," he snarled, "I'll write rude things all over your school books and superglue your PE kit together."

Dayle was struck dumb with fear. Her eyes bulged and her bottom lip quivered. I felt helpless. In my mind I imagined leaping to her rescue, punching Haig in the face and kicking him to the ground until he pleaded for mercy.

In reality, I stood there like a marble statue and did nothing.

"What are you looking at?" he spat at me.

"I'm not sure," my big mouth said.

Haig immediately forgot all about Dayle and shoved his big nose into my face. It felt squashy and hairy and horrible.

"Are you trying to by funny, or what?" he grunted.

Every last molecule of courage vanished. "Me? Funny? No. Never. Honest, Haig. Not me. Not at all."

"Have you got any money?"

"No."

"Why not?"

"Because I spent it all."

"On what?"

I closed my mouth tight, determined not to confess. Someone like Haig Mullins wouldn't understand my interest in boy band posters, and he certainly wouldn't be impressed by the collection of Fun Spells I buy from the Chief Magician.

Haig snatched the satchel from my shoulder, intent on searching inside it. Horrified, I snatched it back. Haig growled at me like an angry dog. I let him take it.

The school doors opened and the bell rang out just as Dayle and I had started picking my books, pens, and PE kit up off the floor. Haig had taken the sweets Mom had given me for lunch and stomped all over my maths book with his big boots, leaving a muddy footprint across the cover. My Maths teacher, who already thought I was an idiot, was not going to be pleased.

He'd also left me with the parting words, "If I don't get some money off you two by lunch time, I'm going to get mad, and you won't like me when I'm mad."

We didn't like him anyway, but his threat scared us. I had visions of him turning into a roaring monster over his runny mash and non-runny gravy in the dinner hall, his uniform splitting, his already angry face turning green. Fear wound itself around my internal organs and started whimpering.

All morning Dayle and I crept around school like terrified mice, trying to avoid bumping into Haig. Near the end of Cookery class we glanced nervously out of the window and spotted him walking toward the Physics lab. He spotted us spotting him, and laughed, shaking his fist up at us. Dayle let out a little cry. I ducked behind a cooker, knocking off a saucepan, which made another girl drop her perfect soufflé. The teacher made us both write out two hundred lines; *I must not cause mass hysteria during school hours.*

At lunch time we saw him lingering around the jugs of cold custard in the dinner hall, just itching to get his hands around our necks.

"We can either fight him to the death," I said, peering at him through a crack in the door, "Or starve."

We starved.

In the afternoon, Dayle kept bursting into tears during PE lesson, making all the apparatus wet and slippery. Gina Wallis almost broke her neck vaulting over the drenched wooden horse.

I spent the afternoon in Maths. The teacher gave me detention for my messy, footprinted book.

By home time we were both nervous wrecks. We sneaked along the corridors, darting from one doorway to the next, ready to make a run for it should the beast make a sudden appearance.

The sprint down the school driveway seemed to go on forever. Our eyes flitted around like loose marbles, searching for any sign of those steel toecap boots. Our ears strained to catch the sound of his heavy breathing.

Finally, we reached the gates.

And there he was, leaning against the railings with his hand outstretched towards us. "Your money or your life," he said.

Dayle and I looked at one another. Haig stepped closer. We stepped back.

"If I don't get fifty pence off both of you within the next ten seconds, you're history."

I was so nervous I began to giggle. I couldn't help myself. Then my stupid mouth started working on its own and said, "He's obviously been watching too many gangster films?" before I had a chance to stop it.

Dayle didn't laugh. She looked horrified. Haig didn't look too happy either, and grabbed hold of my arm.

"Are you making fun of me?" he rasped.

I pressed my lips together, determined not to let my mouth say anything else.

"Money," he snarled, "I want money."

Suddenly, Dayle screamed, "I'm telling my Mom of you," and began to cry, great globules of tears pouring down her face.

Annoyed by Dayle's howling, Haig pounded my limp body against his brick wall of a chest. Dayle, still sobbing hysterically, reached out and tugged desperately at my one arm, whilst Haig tugged at the other. I felt like a piece of elastic about to snap.

Just then, a little boy appeared from nowhere. The besotted first year sidled up to Dayle with love oozing from his eyes.

"What's up, darling?" his unbroken voice asked.

He put an arm around her waist. Dayle immediately released her grip on my arm and I fell to the ground, bringing Haig down on top of me. Several ribs bent under his weight and I had to make a real effort to keep breathing.

Dayle spun round to the little kid who had dared to touch her, and hissed, "Get lost, you odious little animal!"

The first year didn't seem the least bit bothered. In fact, he seemed quite chuffed that she had spoken to him at all. Looking down at Haig with a face full of innocence, he said, "What are you picking on my girlfriend for?"

Dayle's mouth dropped. "I am *not* your girlfriend!" she shrieked.

"She owes me money," Haig said, dragging himself off me and struggling to his feet. "They both do. Fifty pence each."

"I'll buy them both off you for seventy-five pence," the first year said. "As long as Dayle promises to go out with me."

Dayle was bright red with fury. "How *dare* you try and bargain for my affections," she spluttered, "And I'm worth a *lot* more that seventy-five pence!"

"One pound," Haig insisted.

The lovesick kid hesitated for a moment. He turned to inspect Dayle from the toes of her shoes to the top of her head, before finally deciding.

"Okay," he said, thrusting his hand into his trouser pocket and rummaging amongst the fluff, "You've got yourself a deal, mate."

Haig looked well pleased and held out his hand expectantly. Dayle had, by now, turned purple with rage.

"I'd rather be beaten with a cricket bat full of nails than go out with you," she yelled at the first year. "There's *no way* you're going to buy a date with me off someone else. Exactly what kind of a girl do you think I am?"

With that, she spun round on her heels and stormed off down the road. I took one look at Haig, still standing there with his hand held out for the money, and quickly followed her.

The first year watched us leave. Apparently, when he realised that Dayle wasn't going to fall madly in love with him because he'd saved her from the school bully, he changed his mind. When I glanced nervously over my shoulder, I saw him darting across the road waving the pound coin in the air and laughing.

I also saw Haig stiffen, his upper lip curl away from his face. His bristly head turned towards our hastily departing bodies. Then, with a deep roar, he came after us.

"RUN!" I screamed.

Dayle's pace didn't quicken in the slightest as I raced passed her. "Seventy-five pence," I heard her muttering. "The horrible child actually thought he could buy a date with me for seventy-five pence, can you believe it? The *cheek!*"

"Dayle, he's coming!" I gasped, tugging at her arm whilst, behind us down the road, Haig's huge body got closer and closer. "Dayle, he's coming!"

"I mean," she continued to mutter, "I *might* have considered it for a pound, but *seventy-five pence*? No way!"

Haig was gaining on us. I could hear his heavy boots beating a frantic rhythm on the pavement. My heart started to inflate, my stomach pretended it didn't belong to me any more, and still Dayle kept going on about the cheek of first years these days.

Just when I thought the end had arrived, that all hope for survival was gone, a red car pulled up beside us. Mr Jewit, my

Geography teacher, wound down the passenger window.

"Don't forget your homework tonight, Crystal," he said. "It's very important I get it first thing in the morning, not three weeks late like last time."

"Yes, Mr Jewit."

Out of the corner of my eye I saw Haig stop dead in his tracks. We'd been saved. I never thought I'd be so grateful to see my Geography teacher.

"And try and do more than half a page this time, Crystal," Mr Jewit added.

"Yes, sir. Of course, sir. Hope you have an enjoyable evening, sir. Wasn't the weather just awful today, sir?"

Haig loitered in the background, bouncing from one hefty boot to the other. Mr Jewit quickly grew impatient with my attempt to keep him talking until Haig died of boredom or old age, but I tried to keep him there for as long as possible.

"I really do enjoy Geography," I lied. "You're *such* a *good* teacher, Mr Jewit. What do you think of the climate in southern Spain at this time of the year, sir, and do you think living in a hot country is better or worse than living in a cold one?"

Mr Jewit glared at me. "Can we resume this conversation tomorrow, Crystal, only I have an eight month old son I'd quite like to see grow up, if that's okay with you?"

I blushed and stared down at my feet. Mr Jewit shook his head and pulled away from the kerb. Now there was no one to save us.

Haig was stomping towards us again. Mr Jewit drove up the road a little way, then stopped next to another Geography student. Mr Jewit was very strict about homework. Haig slowed down. I prayed he would be delayed by the entire Geography class all the way up the road.

I pushed Dayle forward. She'd abandoned the subject of money and grotty first years, and was now complaining about homework.

"How are we supposed to find time to go out when we have four tons of homework to do every single night of the week?"

Haig getting closer and closer. Mr Jewit was revving up his engine and driving away. As his car faded into the distance, Haig's plodding footsteps started up again. Closer and closer. Louder and louder. My heart pounded. I began to whimper.

Then I heard something else. Another sound. Something familiar.

It was the dry, hoarse noise of magpies chattering in the distance.

I glanced around and saw Maggie and B.W. visiting relatives in the Ash tree on the corner of Gregory Avenue. I jumped up and down, waving my arms in the air to attract their attention, making a complete fool of myself in the process.

Maggie eventually spotted my impersonation of a windmill and came over on the pretence of picking some tasty morsel off the ground.

"What do you want?" she cawed out of the corner of her beak.

"Do you see him?" I whispered, flicking my head back towards a rapidly descending Haig. "He's after us. Can you stall him while we make a run for it?"

Dayle stopped muttering about homework. She turned to look at me as if I'd suddenly gone mad. "Who are you talking to, Crystal?"

Maggie flew up, startled by the sound of a stranger's voice. For one terrible moment I thought she was going to ignore my plea for help and was about to leave us to our fate.

But, as I finally managed to pull Dayle into a run, I caught sight of her black and white wings swooping low over Haig's head and pooing on him.

CHAPTER THREE

I burst breathlessly into my house and found Mom in the kitchen talking to our other neighbour, Mrs Philpotts. From the starved look in Cuthbert's eyes, the bored pose of Merlina, and the chaotic state of the house, Mom must have been nattering to neighbours all day. Mom always did that when she was upset about something - solving other people's problems when she couldn't solve her own.

"Hello, Crystal," she beamed brightly, "Had a nice day at school?"

The voice was familiar, but the face looked like an American film star. I used to wonder what the neighbours thought of Mom's ever-changing appearance, until I heard one neighbour telling another neighbour that Mrs Ball did wonders with make-up and wigs; "Never looks the same twice," they said.

I threw my satchel on the breakfast counter and opened up the fridge for a drink of milk. The four bottles of milk on the shelf had all turned green with age. The fridge chuckled nastily. It was such a spiteful fridge.

"I was just telling Mrs Philpotts about my university degree in medicine," Mom said. "Be an angel, Crystal, and nip up into the attic for me, would you?"

"The attic?" I muttered, furiously slamming the fridge door shut. The fridge whimpered in pain and then growled a rude word. I ignored it. "What do you want me to go up into the attic for?"

"To fetch my medical books," Mom winked. "I'm sure I have

a really good remedy for arthritis somewhere. Poor Mrs Philpotts suffers terribly from arthritis, don't you, dear."

Mrs Philpotts expression turned into instant agony, and she held up her wrinkled, knobbly hands for me to see. It must be awful to be old, I thought.

"Go on then, Crystal," Mom urged.

I sighed heavily and stomped back out of the kitchen. Mom was about to cast one of her Really Useful spells again. Sometimes it was boring being the terribly nice daughter of a terribly nice witch. Oh to cast the odd bad spell once in a while.

I passed Cuthbert in the hallway. He was curled up in his bed under the stairs looking very sorry for himself. "She hasn't fed me again today, you know," he moaned.

"I'll open up a tin for you in a minute."

"A tin?" he grumbled. "Not another tin full of artificial additives and unidentifiable bits of meat. Whatever happened to freshly cooked grub, like steak and chicken?"

"You're lucky," Merlina mewed, delicately licking at her paws as she balanced on the end of the banister rail. "All I ever get is fish heads and tails. No self-respecting tom cat will come near me with breath like mine."

"It isn't your bad breath that makes tom cats run a mile," Cuthbert barked, "It's because you're so *ugly*."

In the blink of an eye, Merlina jumped down off the banister rail, streaked across to Cuthbert, and sank her newly washed claws into his nose. Cuthbert growled, all the hairs on his back standing up on end. Merlina leapt back up onto the banister and hissed down at him. A glittering spell flew out of the kitchen and clamped both their mouths shut.

Leaving my thankfully mute pets glaring silently at each other, I clambered up into the attic. It was piled tile-high with boxes, old furniture, and all my old childhood toys. A thriving population of spiders spun their webby homes in between it all. I accidentally broke a few as I stumbled passed.

"Oi, mind where you're going!" a large spider with a teeny-tiny voice screeched, bouncing up and down on its thin hairy legs.

"It took me three whole days to make that web, and you just barge right through it without any care or consideration."

"Sorry," I said.

"Sorry's no good, is it," the spider yelled. "Where am I going to live now that you've destroyed my home?"

"Build another one."

"Build another one, she says. Have you any idea how long it takes to build a really good web like that?"

"Three days?"

For a moment the spider looked surprised and confused by my answer. Then it huffed and scuttled off to the other side of the attic, where I heard it whispering nasty things about me to some woodworms.

There was an old trunk in the far corner. Mom kept all of her precious possessions in it, including her battered wand which she said was old-fashioned these days.

I opened up the lid. It creaked and sent several mice scampering off into the shadows. The *Book of Magic Spells* was easy to find because it glowed green in the dark. I carefully lifted it out and considered having a peek inside, but resisted the temptation because spell-casting wasn't officially allowed until I was older, after I'd learned all the rules and regulations Mom took absolutely no notice of.

I tucked the book under my arm and was about to close the lid, when I noticed something shining next to the vampire doll Uncle Dracula had given me for my fifth birthday. At the bottom of the trunk, next to my baby photographs and Mom's pointed hat, was a book. An ordinary drawing book. Ordinary, except it had five raised diamonds on the cover. Four twinkled like bright stars, another was dull and didn't twinkle at all.

Curious, I opened it up. On the first page was an unsteady drawing of some hairy monster with big red eyes and a wobbly mouth. It looked vaguely familiar, like something I'd seen before. Maybe, I thought, it was a picture of some distant relative of mine. I took it downstairs to show Mom.

"Who's this?" I asked, after Mrs Philpotts had gone home to

take some purple pills Mom had given her.

"That's not a *who*," she said, peering over my shoulder at the drawing, "That's a *what*."

"Okay, *what* is it?"

"It's a monster you drew when you were little." Mom's eyes misted over and she turned all sloppy. "You were such a talented child, always drawing things, always making things up. You quickly got bored with your ordinary toys, so Dad suggested we give you this book."

"Wow!" I scoffed. "It obviously kept me occupied for hours. There's only one picture in it."

"It's a magic book," Mom said.

"Magic?"

"Yes. Each page is a wish. You were supposed to draw five pictures of the things you wanted the most, and they would become real."

"And I drew a monster?"

"I'm afraid so. You were hysterical when it suddenly appeared in the living room."

"I'm not surprised. It's awful."

"No it's not," Mom cooed, tenderly taking the book from my hands, "Its lovely. A brilliant work of art for a three year old."

I raised my eyes to the ceiling. Parents can be so embarrassing sometimes. When I looked down again, I saw the four bright stars sparkling between Mom's long, black fingernails.

"So, if I only used one wish," I said, as casually as I could manage, "Does that mean there's still four wishes left?"

Mom quickly clutched the book to her chest. "You're not having it," she said.

"But I only want to use the clean pages."

"There's plenty of paper around the house for you to draw on."

"But maybe there's a little bit of magic left. Magic keeps for a long time, doesn't it? Oh, *please*, Mom," I begged, "Let me see if it still works."

Mom firmly shook her head. "You'd be drawing all sorts of

things a three year old would never think of."

"I'd keep it simple, honest. It's such a shame to waste perfectly good magic."

"It's not wasted, Crystal. It'll keep perfectly well until my grandchildren arrive."

"But Mom - !"

"No, and that's my final word on the matter."

Mom headed towards the kitchen door with the book still clutched tight to her body. "I'll put this somewhere safe so you won't get into mischief," she said. "Your father warned me to get rid of it years ago, but I couldn't bear to part with your lovely picture."

She glided elegantly down the hallway, her feet two inches off the floor. At the bottom of the stairs she tilted sideways, rested her head on her arm, and drifted up to the top in a horizontal recline. Mom could be very lazy at times.

As soon as she was out of sight I turned to Merlina, who was mercilessly teasing Cuthbert with a tin of unopened dog food.

"Follow her," I said to my devoted black cat. "Find out where she's hiding that book."

"No," Merlina mewed.

"Oh, go on."

"Can't you see I'm busy trying to get some response from this dead animal you insist on keeping in the hallway?"

"I'll buy you a fresh piece of fish with my pocket money on Friday if you do me this one favour."

Merlina considered this for a moment, then rolled the tin towards Cuthbert, banging him hard on the nose. He yelped. Merlina said, "Okay," and shot up the stairs before he had a chance to retaliate.

Moments later, she streaked back down again. "Dressing table, bottom drawer, underneath the magic herb tin and the solid gold, diamond-encrusted bar she uses as a paperweight."

"Thanks," I said.

"Fish," she said.

"Friday," I said.

But I already knew that, by Friday, Merlina would have forgotten all about the fish and I could buy some more Fun Spells instead.

Later, while Mom was busy watching the television news and making lists of millionaires and worthy charities, I sneaked upstairs to her bedroom. I took the book out of her drawer and hid it under my mattress. Mom never makes beds.

I could barely get to sleep that night thinking about the things I could wish for. There was so much I wanted. I figured that, as they were only baby wishes, I couldn't save the world from starvation or war, so I had four whole wishes all to myself.

Bringing Dad home was top priority, of course. I missed him a lot, and so did Mom. I knew she cried herself to sleep some nights because I had seen the damp patches all over her bedroom ceiling. I would draw a picture of my Dad at home, so he could stay with us forever and never have to haunt again.

I'd get rid of Haig Mullins, too. Nobody calls me Glassy and gets away with it. I would have to think up some really awful punishment for him.

Then I might draw myself having dinner with the handsomest and youngest Master Magician in wizard history, Bloodthorn Thunderbluster Maze III. He'd fall madly in love with me, we'd get married, live on a sprawling ranch in America and ride around on horses all day holding hands.

"Mrs Crystal Maze," I said out loud. It sounded good.

After that I might get some famous historical genius like Einstein, or maybe Elon Musk, to help me with my homework. Or, better still, I could make the Prime Minister pass a law that banned homework altogether.

And I wanted a whole new wardrobe of clothes, and some fancy jewellery, and a nice mansion in the country, and pets that didn't answer back all the time.

I wanted *so* much. And now I could have it all.

Excitement kept me awake until the early hours of the morning. I overslept and was late getting ready for school. I had to run around the house like an Olympic athlete frantically searching for my satchel and shoes.

Cuthbert was suspiciously helpful and offered to wash my face with his rough tongue. Then I found my shoes in his bed, both chewed to pieces. Cuthbert and his rough tongue slunk off to hide in a cupboard.

I repaired my shoes with a bit of illicit magic, but magic doesn't like to be bothered first thing in the morning and my shoes turned from black to a sort of yucky yellow. I tried to magic up some new shoes, but ended up with plastic sandals, so I had to wear the yucky yellow ones.

I took the book to school with me and showed Dayle. Dayle knows my Mom is a witch, that I have pets that answer back, that my Dad is a ghost, but she found it hard to believe that an ordinary-looking drawing book would grant me four wishes.

"Get real!" she laughed, as we sat inside a classroom during the wet break time.

"Honest, Dayle. Whatever I draw in this book will become real."

"Prove it," she said.

"How?"

"Make something horrible happen to Haig Mullins. It's the only way I'll be convinced."

I tutted, hesitated, bit my lip a bit, then opened up the book. There were so many possibilities, so many ghastly revenges I could scribble on that blank page.

For endless minutes I sat chewing the end of my pencil with Dayle breathing heavily over my shoulder. Finally, a scene began to form in my mind, a really ugly revenge for a really ugly school bully.

Eagerly, I put pencil to paper. The end broke off. Pulling my satchel onto my lap, I was about to search for my pencil sharpener when Dayle impatiently thrust a biro into my hand and rasped, "Just draw!"

Slowly, carefully, I sketched the shape of a large body with spiky hair that only vaguely resembled Haig Mullins. Then I drew thick lines all around it to represent a metal cage.

"Art isn't your best subject, is it?" Dayle grumbled.

Ignoring her, I put a variety of evil-looking monsters with huge fangs all around the cage. Then, in a mad fit of inspiration, Dayle insisted I draw a jagged horizon in the background and colour the sky pink to make it look like a Martian landscape.

When the page was filled and the picture complete, I held it up and studied my masterpiece.

"When will it happen?" Dayle asked breathlessly.

"I don't know."

"How do you make it happen?" she asked.

"I don't know that, either."

Dayle huffed in disgust. "Our whole break time wasted on some silly drawing, and for what? For nothing!"

"It'll work," I said. "I just don't know how, or when."

I closed the book and stared at the four bright stars on the cover. "All I know is that every time a wish is granted one of these lights go out."

"One's gone out already," Dayle enthused.

"I used that one when I was three years old. It wasn't quite the playmate I expected but ... oh, never mind. There were four stars glowing when we started and there's still four glowing now."

Dayle fell back into her chair and frowned. "It's a joke, right?" she growled. "You've been winding me up all this time, haven't you?"

Determined to convince her, I pointed at the stars with the tip of my finger. "When one of these goes out," I insisted, "Our wish will come true."

And I prodded at one of the stars. It flickered, and went dull. Dayle and I both sat bolt upright in our chairs and stared at it. I suddenly felt very frightened.

"Do you think - ?" Dayle began.

"I hope not," I breathed.

Somewhere in the distance, a loud scream echoed down one of the long, dark corridors of the school.

Dayle turned to me with wide eyes. "That scream," she said, clutching my arm, "It sounded ... it sounded just like Haig

Mullins."

I began to shake. With trembling hands, I opened up the drawing book. My blood turned to ice as I stared at the picture I had drawn.

It *had* sounded like Haig Mullins screaming. And one of the stars *had* gone out.

It could only mean that our wish had been granted, that the thing we had drawn had become real.

Was Haig Mullins, the school bully and the blight of our lives, now trapped in a cage surrounded by monsters on some strange planet?

It didn't bear thinking about.

"Has it happened?" Dayle asked anxiously. "Have we really made something awful happen to Haig Mullins?"

"I ... I think so."

I felt the blood drain from my face, and watched Dayle turn white. We held each other's hands tightly and willed ourselves not to panic.

When registration was taken in the form class that afternoon, Haig Mullins was noticeably absent. There was a serene, tranquil silence that prompted our teacher to ask after him.

"I think he went home," someone said.

"Are you sure?" the teacher asked.

"No, Miss."

"Did you actually see him leave school?"

"No, Miss."

"Then what makes you think he went home?"

"Well, Miss, he's not here, is he."

Dayle was on the verge of tears. "You have to do something," she whispered. "You have to bring him back. Oh," she wailed, "I should never have let you talk me into it in the first place."

"It wasn't *my* idea!"

"There's no time to argue," she rasped. "Just bring him back before we get into serious trouble and *before* Haig gets really, really mad. Bring him back, Crystal. *Bring him back now!*"

"I don't know how."

Dayle snatched up her bag, stood up, and went and sat down next to Fiona Harrison on the other side of the classroom. My so-called best friend had abandoned me in my greatest hour of need.

Haig didn't turn up at school the next day. Or the day after that. There was a rumour going around that he'd run away from home because his parents wouldn't give him more pocket money. Dayle and I knew better.

It was only our mutual fear that brought us back together again in the girl's toilet one break time. Dayle was scared of being caught, of someone finding out what we had done.

"Ask your Mom what to do," she demanded. "Get the wish reversed. Just *do* something, Crystal, to bring him back before someone finds out what we've done."

"I can't ask my Mom!"

"Why not?"

"Because she'd freak out and tell my Dad, and he'll ground me for months and take away all my Fun Spells."

Dayle screwed up her face and hissed, "Are you saying you won't bring Haig back because you don't want to lose your Fun Spells? Crystal, you're so *selfish*!"

"You don't understand," I cried. "If I don't buy Fun Spells off the Chief Magician every week, he'll get suspicious and come round to the house to find out what's wrong. If he discovers what I've done, he'll blame Mom and empty all the magic in her magic account, and if Mom doesn't have the magic to cook and clean and change her face every ten minutes she'll have a nervous breakdown and then Dad will - "

"Okay, okay," Dayle said, "I get the point. But if we can't ask your Mom for help, what can we do?"

"I don't know, Dayle. I really don't know."

It was all such a mess.

CHAPTER FOUR

One night after school, a few days after Haig Mullins' disappearance, we went up to Dayle's bedroom to discuss the crisis.

"He might be dead," Dayle said - always one to look on the bright side.

I shook my head. "No, it's white magic. If you try to cast a bad spell to hurt someone, it comes back like a boomerang and turns you into a frog."

I glanced down the length of my body as I lay sprawled across Dayle's bed, checking for any sign of green skin or gills.

"But drawing Haig Mullins on a strange planet *was* a bad spell, wasn't it, Crystal?"

I considered this for a moment. "I guess the drawing book gives wishing spells, the kind children use. They taught us in The Infant School for Witches' Offspring that wishing spells aren't protected like magic spells because children rarely think of nasty things to wish for."

"But you did."

"Yeah. I know."

"Perhaps we shouldn't try to bring him back," Dayle said. "He'll be really mad by now, and who knows what he'll do to us. And we'll get into trouble if he tells anyone what we did to him."

"He won't know it was *us* who sent him hurtling off into deepest, darkest space."

"Are you sure?"

"Well, no, I'm not absolutely certain, but we can't leave him there forever."

"Why not?" Dayle asked.

"Because it's not a nice thing to do to someone, is it?"

"Okay, so we'll bring him back."

"Fine. How?"

Dayle tutted irritably. "Well, how did you get rid of that monster you drew when you were three years old?"

"I'm not sure. It's all very vague."

"*Think*, Crystal. It's important."

I frowned, and grimaced, and closed my eyes tight. "I remember crawling under a chair and screaming my lungs out. And I remember this horrible hairy creature chasing after me. And then ... and then ... "

"Yes? Then what happened?"

"Mom beat it off with a rolling pin and made it disappear."

"HOW?" Dayle shrieked.

"Mom has her own special brand of magic, bought cheap in a sale at Strangebury's."

"Great!" she snorted. "All we have to do is nip down to the nearest supermarket and buy a gross of magic spells."

"I don't think they have them on offer any more, Dayle. Besides, big spells are very expensive."

Dayle peered at me strangely for a moment, as though trying to decide whether she should take me seriously or not. While she was piercing me with her eyeballs, I could see her brain shift into a different gear.

Suddenly she stood up, her gaze moving to a dirt mark on the wall, and her face took on an intelligent, thoughtful expression - no easy task for Dayle. I waited expectantly, hopefully, for her mind-boggling solution to our problem.

"What if we tear the page out of the book and burn it?" she asked.

"That will seal the spell," I sighed, disappointed. "We'll never be able to bring Haig back once the spell is sealed."

"Then what *are* we going to do?"

"I don't know, do I! Perhaps if we stop thinking about it so much we'll think of something, if you know what I mean. We're trying too hard and probably ignoring the obvious answer in the process."

Dayle sat down at her dressing table, nodding her head in agreement. "Right, we'll make our minds a complete blank and not think of anything at all."

"Should be easy for you."

"Shut your mouth!"

I rolled over onto my back on the bed and counted the cracks in the ceiling. Dayle spun slowly on the dressing table chair and surveyed her messy room, winding a lock of hair around her finger. She came face to face with her reflection in the mirror and all concentration was taken up with a close inspection of her features.

"I hate my hair," she said, picking up a brush and trying to drag it through her frizzy mop. "And my eyes are too small, my nose it too big, and my lips aren't pouty enough."

Her non-pouty lips suddenly stretched into a huge, gooey smile. I knew what was coming before she'd even uttered the words.

"Don't ask," I said.

"But it will only be *one* wish from the book, Crystal. You'll still have two left all to yourself. And it would certainly take our minds off our problem for a while, wouldn't it?"

"No, no, and no. There is *no way* I can make you look beautiful, Dayle."

"Thanks a bunch!" she huffed. "Don't try and flatter me or anything, will you? Just come right to the point and tell me I'm ugly!"

"I'm sorry," I wailed, burying my head in a pillow. "I didn't mean it like that."

Her voice went all soft and mushy again. "One tiny, itsy-bitsy wish will last me for the rest of my life, Crystal. I've always fancied being a famous film star, and I *can* if you make me look really gorgeous. Oh go on, Crystal," she begged shamelessly. "Be a pal. I swear I'll never ask you to do anything else ever again as long as I

_ "

"No," I said firmly, "I only have three wishes left, and I haven't brought my Dad back home yet, or made Bloodthorn Thunderbluster Maze III, the handsomest wizard there ever was, fall madly in love with me."

"What's the love of one man worth compared to a lifetime of fame and fortune?" she said dramatically. "I think you're being *very* selfish, Crystal. You're *supposed* to be my best friend. I *always* share my things with *you*."

"That's not true!" I sat bolt upright on the bed and glared at her fiercely. "What about that time you wouldn't let me wear your blue angora jumper for the school disco, and *all* those times you wouldn't let me borrow any of your DVDs in case I scratched them or used them as coasters, or that time when - ?"

"Okay, okay." She lowered her head in mock shame. "I apologise from the bottom of my heart for all the nasty things I've ever done to you. But Crystal," she whined, "If we make another wish we'll be able to figure out how to reverse it, won't we?"

I digested her words. She continued to persuade me. "If you draw me and make me look beautiful, then you can work out how to make me ugly again. And, if you can do that, you can bring Haig back as well."

I had to admit she had a point. It might just work.

"And when we have Haig back," she continued, "You can make me beautiful again as my reward for being so brilliant."

"But," I spluttered, "That will be a waste of *two* perfectly good wishes."

"A waste!" she huffed. "Isn't it worth it to bring Haig back?"

Was it? I wondered. Visions of Bloodthorn down on his knees begging me to marry him rapidly faded from my mind. I sighed. I tutted. I thought of my Dad still stuck in some draughty Scottish castle and sighed again.

"I'll give you ten percent of everything I earn from my acting career," Dayle said. "You'll be rich beyond your wildest dreams."

"White witches aren't allowed to accept payment for their magic," I said. "It's against the rules."

"Then I'll let you share my huge mansion in Beverly Hills with me."

"I'd much rather stay here with Mom and Dad."

"They can come and live with us, too."

"I don't think Beverly Hills will be very happy about having a witch and a ghost as neighbours, or be too pleased about the hoards of visiting vampire relatives dropping by for cocktails by the slime infested swimming pool."

"You're *so* hard to please!"

We sat in silence for a moment. I knew in my heart of hearts that Dayle was probably right. Casting another spell was the only way to find out how to bring Haig back, and if that spell made Dayle beautiful, then what did it matter if Bloodthorn ran off and married someone else? Sob.

Eventually, after much deliberation, I finally agreed to her demands. Dayle got all excited, jumping up and down and waving her arms in the air. Then she sat beside me on the bed, handed me a sharpened pencil, and eagerly described exactly how she wanted to look.

The resulting picture was hardly a work of art. Far from having a head of thick golden curls, the hair looked like a shredded wheat balanced on top of a warped ping-pong ball head. The eyes were like saucers. The chest - which Dayle insisted I make Ultra-Mega-Extra-Large - were like enormous beach balls sticking out of her body. And I couldn't get the mouth right. Dayle wanted to have lips that looked full and inviting, but they looked like a pair of pink car tyres.

Even the shape of the body was way out of proportion - a lumpy sack of potatoes on stick legs - but Dayle seemed absolutely delighted with it. I couldn't understand why.

"It's not meant to be perfect, is it," she said, suddenly becoming an expert on drawing books. "After all, that one you did of Haig Mullins was only a sketch, but it still worked."

"Only because we emphasised his physical appearance so the spell would recognise him. We didn't *change* the way he looked, Dayle."

My heart went all heavy at the thought of Haig still suffering on some grotty planet. Dayle seemed to have forgotten all about him as she greedily anticipated future fame and fortune with her stunning good looks.

"I don't think we ought to do this," I said. "At least not until I've done a few years of training at an art school. Perhaps we should tell my Mom after all."

"No! We can't do that! We have to solve this by ourselves, prove that we can do it without any adults poking their noses in. By the way, can you make my nose just a *little* bit smaller?"

"But what if it goes wrong? Again!" I scribbled over the button nose, turning it into two huge nostrils in the middle of a hideous face. "My drawing is the pits, Dayle. You might end up looking worse that you do now."

"What do you mean, worse than I look now?" she hissed.

I shrugged my shoulders and mumbled yet another apology. At any other time Dayle would have given me hell for making such comments about her appearance, but now she forgave me on the spot. If she fell out with me, I almost heard her thinking, she'd never be beautiful.

Dayle glanced at the picture again. "I'm telling you, Crystal, it *will* work. You've drawn all the things I want changed, and that's all that matters. Just think," she beamed, eyes wide and sparkling, "I'll actually have boobs that people can *see*."

I still wasn't happy about it. Nobody could have boobs as big as the ones I'd drawn and still be able to walk.

"Come on," she urged, "I'll take full responsibility. If it doesn't work, I won't blame you in the slightest."

"I'll bet! You're not the most forgiving person in the world, are you?"

"What do you mean?" she pouted.

"When Ruth Gordon tripped you up during a basketball game, you threw the ball in her face and made her nose bleed."

"That was an accident!"

"It was deliberate, Dayle. I was there. I saw it. And I dread to think what you'll do to me if this spell turns out wrong."

"Not a thing, Crystal, I swear. Come on. Please? Pretty please?"

"Are you sure about this? Really, absolutely, positively sure?"

"Yes. Now do it!"

"We really ought to give it a bit more thought, not rush into anything."

Dayle's patience snapped right about then. Twisting her thin mouth into a furious scowl and squinting her eyes into slits, she hissed, "If you don't go through with it right now, I'll never speak to you again for as long as I live."

"Is that a threat or a promise?"

"How dare you! After what I'm putting myself through to help you and Haig!"

"You're not doing it for me or for Haig," I said. "You're doing it for yourself."

"I am not! I'm being very brave and selfless, allowing myself to be mutilated by magic so that you can find out how to reverse the spell and bring Haig back."

I took a deep breath and was about to tell her that being made to look impossibly beautiful was hardly a great act of self-sacrifice, when she yelled, "JUST GET ON WITH IT, FOR GOODNESS SAKE!"

Angry, and hoping she'd get all she deserved, I touched the star on the cover of the drawing book. The light went out. I looked up. I saw Dayle floating down to the floor like a feather in a breeze.

She was as thin as a piece of paper. She *was* a piece of paper. And she looked exactly the same as the drawing in every way, right down to the huge clubbed feet.

"Help!" she screamed through tissue lips.

I fell down beside her and tried to pick her up, but she was so thin I was terrified I might rip her. I'd turned my best friend into a piece of paper, a comic drawing, a *cartoon*! There was nothing remotely realistic about her, not even the muffled cardboard voice.

"Do something," she cried.

"What?"

"Oh Crystal, I can't go through life looking like this." A single confetti tear appeared in the corner of her saucer-sized eye.

"People will laugh. I'll get blown away or torn up. I'll be *recycled*! There's no way I'll become rich and famous being a black and white drawing."

"Oh I don't know," I said, "The Disney film studio might be interested, and there's a big demand for really skinny models, and you can't get any skinnier than this."

"This is not time to be funny!" she hissed. "Change me back, NOW!"

"It may have slipped your memory," I told her, "But we've already had this problem once before, with Haig, remember? The thing is, Dayle, *I don't know how to change you back.*"

"Then you better think of something, and quick." She started crying again.

"Don't do that," I said. "You'll make yourself go all soggy and turn into paper mache."

Dayle bawled even louder. I jumped back onto the bed, picked up the drawing book, and vainly searched the pages for inspiration. There weren't even any operating instructions included at the back.

"What should I do?" I cried.

"Rub it out," she said. "Rub the picture out."

"Where can I find a rubber?"

"LOOK FOR ONE!"

So I did, in the drawers, in the wardrobe, the cupboards, and amongst the piles of junk on the dressing table.

"Your bedroom is a tip," I told her, peering at the three inches of fluff beneath her bed. "Doesn't your mother make you clear up the debris occasionally? There's even a mouldy cheese sandwich under here, Dayle. That's *really* disgusting."

"Never mind about that, just find a pencil rubber. And fast, I can feel a crease coming on."

I eventually located a toy doll with a rubber face, and frantically attacked the picture with it. The doll's nose broke off and one of the glass eyes fell out, but the drawing did eventually begin to fade.

Dayle, still lying like an outstretched poster on the floor, began to change. Her hair turned back into yellow straw, her eyes shrunk into tiny peepholes, and her arms and legs filled out into real flesh again.

She stood up unsteadily. "I have never been so scared in my entire life," she breathed. "I thought I was going to be stuck like that forever."

As she collapsed onto the bed next to me, her hair fell back from her face. I noticed her ears instantly. They were thin and white and very large. I sucked in my breath and tried not to make any reference to elephants.

"Now we know what to do about Haig Mullins," she said smugly. "I told you my little plan would work, didn't I?"

We looked at each other. It was hard for me to keep a straight face when her ears were flapping backwards and forwards like a giant butterfly trying to take off. But at least we didn't have to worry about Haig being suck on a strange planet surrounded by horrible monsters any more.

And yet, we both felt reluctant to bring him back. Attacks in the playground, hair pulling, teasing and threats, it would all be the same as it was before, perhaps even worse after his enforced visit to a hostile planet.

"I don't suppose we have a choice really, do we?" Dayle sighed.

"No, I suppose not."

"Go on then, get it over with."

"The peace and quiet was nice while it lasted."

"Yeah, and we can always draw him back on the planet again if he gets too nasty." Dayle put a hand on my arm and looked deep into my eyes. "And you don't have to worry about wasting another wish to make me look beautiful, Crystal. Being a cartoon character once is enough for anybody."

I nodded. I smiled. I started rubbing out the picture of Haig Mullins using the remnants of the dolls face.

Only it wouldn't rub out. We hadn't drawn Haig with a pencil. We'd used a biro, and no amount of rubbing would make the ink disappear.

We couldn't bring him back after all.

CHAPTER FIVE

It was no good. There was nothing else for it. We couldn't put it off any longer. With Dayle crying her eyes out and me thinking of all the awful things that were about to happen, we went round to my house and told my Mom.

"YOU DID *WHAT*?" she shrieked.

Dayle and I cowered at the kitchen table, waiting for the worst, which wasn't long in coming. I'd never seen my mother lose her temper before, like *really* lose it.

She stood leaning up against the kitchen sink, her eyes wide and her mouth hanging open. Somewhere in the distance a low rumbling noise started. It grew louder, came closer, until we thought the house would fall down around our ears - Dayle's *paper* ears.

Cuthbert raised his head, whimpered, then bolted out the back door. Merlina arched her back, hissed, and jumped half way up the kitchen wall, where she hung with her claws around a light switch.

"YOU SENT A *CHILD* INTO *SPACE*!" Mom roared above the sound of cracking thunder.

Too afraid to speak, Dayle and I meekly nodded our heads.

"YOU SENT A POOR, INNOCENT CHILD INTO THE UNKNOWN?"

"Well," Dayle quivered, "I wouldn't say he was totally innocent. Quite a few victims at school would gladly have *paid* to send him where he is now."

"SHUT UP!" Mom screamed.

"Yes, Mrs Ball. Of course, Mrs Ball. Anything you say, Mrs Ball. I'm really, really sorry, Mrs - "

"That's enough," I whispered. "There's only so much grovelling you can do at a time like this."

Mom raised her arms in the air and screamed through gritted teeth. The back door flew open, revealing Cuthbert cringing with fear by the dustbins. A lightning bolt struck one of the metal lids, sending sparks flying into the air and making Cuthbert scurry off to the safety of the garden shed.

A howling wind blew though the kitchen. Lightning flashed across the ceiling as thunder rocked the walls of the house. The noise was deafening. Dayle threw her head down onto the table and covered it with her arms, crying and sobbing.

"We didn't mean to do it, Mom," I wailed. "It was only meant to be a joke. We just wanted to teach him a lesson, that's all. He's such a nasty boy - "

"THAT IS *NO* EXCUSE FOR DUMPING HIM ON A MONSTER-INFESTED PLANET, CRYSTAL!"

Sparkling light flashed from the tips of her long fingernails and bounced off the top of the cooker like fireworks, making the cooker flinch. Mom was *really* mad. The kettle flew up into the air, spun around, and crashed down on the floor. Teacups and saucers shot off shelves and smashed against the walls.

"WHAT DID I SEND YOU TO MAGIC SCHOOL FOR, CRYSTAL, IF NOT TO LEARN ALL THE RULES?" Mom raged.

"But *you* break all the rules, Mom."

"THAT IS *NOT* THE POINT. I MAKE *GOOD* SPELLS. I DO *NOT* MAKE PEOPLE VANISH OFF THE FACE OF THE EARTH BECAUSE THEY'VE UPSET ME."

"I know. I'm sorry."

Balls of coloured light streaked around the kitchen, splattering against the windows and vanishing with a hiss. Mom's eyes were so wide I thought they might actually pop out of her head. Her face was bright red, her long hair stood up on end and spread out across the ceiling, and her robe flapped angrily around her body.

"What can we do, Mom?" I sobbed. "Can you bring him back?"

Another crack of thunder drowned her words. The cooker joined in the chaos by opening and slamming shut its door, and the fridge began jumping up and down, tossing ice-cubes out of the freezer. Merlina slowly sipped down the wall, leaving deep scratch-marks in the wallpaper. Outside, Cuthbert howled in terror from the shed.

"Mom?"

She said something I couldn't hear. Lightning struck Melina's tail and she flashed across the floor and jumped through the window. The sound of splintered glass added to the noise.

Mom said something else, and I still couldn't hear her. She frowned, rolled her eyes to the scorched ceiling, and dropped her arms to her side.

"THAT WILL DO," she screamed at no one in particular.

The thunder and lightning stopped immediately, the cooker kept still, the kitchen utensils dropped from the air like rocks, and the electric blender crawled behind the bread bin. Suddenly, thankfully, glorious silence reigned in the kitchen once more. There was just the clinking of ice cubes as the fridge continued to flick them merrily across the room, but Mom froze it with a cold glare and it stopped.

With her fury spent, Mom calmly patted her hair into place and smoothed down her robe. She looked first at me, then at Dayle. Slowly, she crossed the room and sat down at the table. Her face still looked fierce and furious, but there was also a softness in her green eyes.

"Okay," she said, "Tell me everything."

So we did; all about Haig picking on Dayle and being the school bully, how we'd drawn a nasty picture to get rid of him, and even how we'd turned Dayle into a piece of paper.

"You have been busy, haven't you?" Mom frowned.

I lowered my head.

"But you can bring him back, can't you, Mrs Ball?" Dayle asked.

Mom tutted and shook her head. "I'm not sure," she said. "We're not really supposed to mess around with anybody else's magic, and I've never been very good at reversing spells anyway."

That was true. I suddenly felt nervous.

"But you must be able to do *something*," Dayle cried.

"My husband might know what to do."

"But Dad's in Scotland," I said, "And we're not allowed to visit him."

Mom stared at me, pursing her lips. "I know we're not *supposed* to visit him," she said, "But you're not *supposed* to use white magic for bad spells either, are you?"

"Does that mean ... ?"

Mom stood up. "Yes," she said, "We're going to ask him what we can do to bring that poor child back to earth."

Dayle looked at me. I looked at her. "Poor child?" we both said together.

Mom came round to our side of the table and Dayle cringed, expecting to be clobbered or electrified with magic. Instead, Mom reached out and draped one of Dayle's enormous paper ears over her fingers. "We're definitely going to have to do something about these, my dear," she said.

"About what?" Dayle's hands flew up to the sides of her head. Her face crumpled, pieced itself back together again, and then it turned to fix me with a look of both anger and horror. "WHY DIDN'T YOU TELL ME YOU'D TURNED MY EARS INTO SHEETS OF PAPER?" she snarled.

"I thought they looked rather fetching, actually."

"Don't worry about them," Mom soothed, as she stopped Dayle reaching for my neck. "We can soon cut them down to size."

"Cut them!" she screamed, as Mom took a pair of scissors from a drawer. "You're not going to *cut* them, are you?"

"It won't hurt. Honestly. A little snip here, a little snip there. Nobody will ever notice the difference, although you'll never be able to wear earrings again, I'm afraid, oir go swimming."

"Couldn't you just change them back to the way they were before, Mom?" I asked. "You know, real flesh and blood ears."

"Oh yes," she giggled, "Of course. Why didn't I think of that?"

Dayle almost fainted with relief. With one sparkling flash of magic from Mom's fingertips her ears went back to normal.

On Mom's instructions, Dayle then ran home to ask her mother if she could come with us to visit my Dad. Dayle neglected to tell her mother that my Dad was a ghost haunting some castle in Scotland, so her mother allowed her to go. Dayle came back wearing a thick waterproof fishing jacket, a woolly hat, two pairs of gloves, three scarves, and a huge pair of fur-lined boots.

"Didn't your mother suspect anything?" I asked, as Dayle stood in the middle of our kitchen looking like an Eskimo expecting a snowstorm.

"She did look a little surprised when I asked her where my thermal underwear was, but she thinks all teenagers are obliged to act strange from time to time, just to keep their parents on their toes."

"You wear thermal underwear?" I giggled.

I would have broken in a laugh at that moment, but Dayle punched me in the ribs with her padded fists before I had a chance to draw breath.

Mom came back downstairs after a furtive rummage in her cobweb-infested wardrobe. She was wearing her own face and was carrying her velvet black cloak with the silver-embroidered stars.

"Should I wear my matching black hat with this, or not?" she asked.

"Will you need your matching black hat?" I asked.

"No, but your Dad likes it."

"Then wear it."

"But I feel so silly with it on, so old-fashioned."

"Then don't wear it."

"But - "

"Mom! Let's just *go*."

Dayle stood closely at my side looking pensive and terrified. "How?" she gulped, "How, exactly, are we going to get to Scotland?"

"How do you think?" I grinned.

The colour drained from her face. "I've no idea," she said, "But I have a nasty suspicion we *won't* be catching a train, or a bus, or going by car, if we had a car."

"How do witches normally get around, Dayle?"

Her eyes widened. "No. You don't mean ... Not by ... "

Mom came over and patted her heartily on the back. "Don't worry, dear," she said, immediately making Dayle worry, "There's plenty of room on my broomstick for three, and I've never lost a passenger yet. Well, except for that time I gave all those goblins a lift home from a beastly birthday bash. They dragged the swamp for days afterwards but they never found them. Rumour has it they eloped with a couple of ghosts from the most haunted house in Britain, which didn't please the locals very much as they did a roaring trade selling spooky gifts to the tourists."

Dayle attempted a smile. She looked at Mom, then at me, then back at Mom again. "You're joking, right?" she said. "You can't be serious. A broomstick? In this day and age?"

Mom pulled a long switch-stick from a cupboard and blew away the cobwebs – the spiders weren't pleased. Dayle fainted dead on the spot. I never knew how difficult it was to drape an unconscious and heaviliy padded body over a broomstick before.

Dayle came round just as we were waiting in the garden for take-off. Mom was up front, with me at the back, wedging Dayle's body between us like a sandwich filling. We were waiting for an airplane to pass over - we'd promised all the airports that we wouldn't fly near any of their aircraft because it distracted the pilots.

"I don't want to go," Dayle whined, struggling to get off.

I grabbed her round the scruff of her fur-lined neck and hissed, "We're in this together, and you're coming with us."

And, at that, Mom took off into the star-speckled sky, singing, "Up, up and away on my beautiful, my beautiful b-room."

When we'd shot up vertically for about half a mile, Dayle made the mistake of looking down at the ground far below us, and let out a horrendous scream that grew louder and louder the higher we got. Mom glanced over her shoulder and told her to shut up before the neighbours complained. The broomstick continued to climb up into the heavens with a shudder and a wobble and a whoosh.

"I can't believe this," Dayle muttered. "This can't be happening to me. It's a dream. A nightmare. I'm not really flying through the night sky on a broomstick with my ex-best friend and her mother."

"And a cat," I said.

If Dayle hadn't been sitting as stiff as a board between us, she might have noticed Merlina hanging down behind us with her claws clinging to the brush end. Merlina hadn't wanted to come along on the trip either, but then, she shouldn't use Mom's broomstick as a scratching post, should she

I pulled the cat up and stuck her onto Dayle's padded back. We flew up higher and higher until the houses below looked like the models on a train set.

"Look," I cried, tapping Dayle on the shoulder. "There's our school."

Dayle looked down and let out another ear-shattering scream. Her cries increased when Mom casually asked if anyone knew the way to Scotland, and it reached ultimate pitch when Mom said she couldn't follow the North star because she couldn't *see* the North star without her glasses.

By a sheer stroke of luck we managed to locate a motorway and found an illuminated sign with *To The North* written on it. We followed it as it zigzagged across the landscape, flying over Birmingham and Manchester, before Mom accidentally took a wrong turn and ended up in Blackpool.

"I want to see the lights," I cried.

Mom hesitated for the briefest moment, then she said, "Oh, alright then, but just a quick peek."

Pushing the broomstick down at the front end, Dayle and I slithered along the handle until we were lined up like bodies on a toast rack behind Mom. Mom swooped low and flew straight up the main street beneath all the illuminations. At the last possible moment, she pulled up towards the full moon, narrowly missing Blackpool tower. The entire hair-raising spectacle had taken all of five seconds.

"I used to be a high-speed flyer in my youth," she cackled.

"All I saw was a blur of bright lights," I complained.

Dayle didn't say anything. She was probably asleep, I thought, and frozen to the broomstick by the cold night air. Or else she'd slipped into a coma.

Finally, by a fortunate run of good luck, we reached Carlisle and flew across the Scottish border just as dawn was beginning to break.

"We'll be spotted in daylight," Mom said. "We'll have to go around the coastline."

And she turned the broomstick a sharp left and headed far out to sea. The sudden manoeuvre caught Dayle off balance and she slithered underneath the pole, hanging upside-down like a bat. She didn't make a noise and made no attempt to right herself again, so I had to haul her back up with Merlina still clinging to her back.

Along with the blazing red sunrise came storm-clouds. The wind blew into a gale, the rain lashed into our faces like sharp pellets, and Mom got blown off course away from the coastline.

"We're lost," she eventually said.

"Nice going, Mom."

"We're going to die," Dayle whined in a strange little voice. "We're going to be lost at sea, never to be found. A watery grave. Ohhhhhh!"

The whinging continued for several minutes, until sheer exhaustion and terror shut her up again. Down below, in the raging sea, I spotted a light flickering up and down on the waves.

"Go and ask that boat the way to dry land," I shouted to Mom.

We dropped out of the sky like a brick and bounced along the water before crashing into the hull of a rusty fishing trawler. Merlina crawled up Dayle's back until she was wrapped around Dayle's head like a huge fur hat. Merlina *hates* water.

We rose up slowly, fighting against the gale-force wind, and found ourselves face-to-face with a swaying fisherman in yellow oilskins standing on deck.

"Excuse me," Mom said sweetly, "We appear to be lost."

The man staggered back a couple of paces and rubbed his eyes with the palms of his hands. When he opened them again, he seemed surprised to still find us there, hovering just outside the boat rails above the raging sea.

"You're a witch!" he gasped.

"Yes, I did know."

"On a broomstick!"

"That's right. How very observant of you."

"A witch, on a broomstick, in the middle of the ocean!"

"To be truthful," Mom said, "I don't normally take this route. I'm not a sea-faring witch, you see, and much prefer dry land. Hence the need for directions."

"I've been out here for too long," the fisherman cried deliriously, wobbling a bit and allowing a wave of salt-water to pour into his open mouth.

"Could you be so kind as to point us in the right direction for Scotland?" Mom asked.

The fisherman appeared to lose all power of speech. His floppy mouth opened and closed like a fish out of water. Then, very slowly, he raised one arm and pointed into the murky distance.

"Thank you so much," Mom said, smiling and turning the broomstick in the direction he had indicated. "By the way," she cried over her shoulder as we flew off, "If you're interested, there's a big shoal of fish over there to the left of your nets."

The fisherman didn't move, didn't speak – a bit like Dayle. As his ship slowly faded behind the sheets of rain, I noticed his bright yellow jacket remained motionless on deck, where he probably remained long after we had disappeared from sight. Some people react very strangely to witches on broomsticks.

Somehow, despite the fisherman's help, the howling wind blew us off course again. When we eventually came to dry land and parked for a while to dry off. I noticed our surroundings looked a little ... unusual.

"I don't think we're in Scotland, Mom."

"Of course we are," she said, shaking the water off her cloak and squeezing Merlina dry. "That nice fisherman told us the way, although I have to say yellow isn't his colour at all. Green would suit him better, I think. It would co-ordinate with his face."

"No, Mom," I insisted, "We're definitely not in Scotland. Scotland is a big place. What we're standing on is commonly referred to as an *island*."

"Ireland?" Dayle whimpered, her eyes growing more blank and glassy by the minute. "We're in Ireland?"

"No, Dayle. Go back to sleep, Dayle."

And she did.

A passing local laughed himself stupid when we stopped and asked him where we were. We couldn't understand a word he said because his accent was so strong. The only word we could make out was Egg.

"Egg?" Mom said. "What is he waffling on about, Crystal? Tell him I don't want breakfast, I want directions."

"Egg," the man repeated, "N'Muck en Rum."

"What country are we in?" Dayle asked me. "That's not English he's speaking, is it?"

The face of Mr Jewit suddenly thudded into my head. Once again, I was grateful for geography.

"We're on *Eigg*," I declared, "A little Scottish island between Muck and Rhum."

"So which way is it to the mainland?" Mom asked the man.

The man gave us a stream of instructions, none of which we understood. Then he pointed, which we did understand, and suddenly we were flying off into the cloudy sky again, bouncing over the water with Mom trying very hard to keep a straight line. The broomstick was tired and wanted to rest.

"It would have been quicker by train," I mumbled, glancing at my watch.

"Train," Dayle whimpered. "Yes, we'll catch the train, a nice safe train on the ground, with no water or rain or wind."

A jagged precipice came into view. Mom levelled off enough to land and read a road sign, which confirmed we were on the right side of the world, at least. All we had to do was find the ruin of a haunted castle.

Mom tried to get the broomstick going again. Having felt solid ground beneath its wood, it positively refused to budge another inch.

"Want rest," its timbers creaked, "Go away."

Mom grabbed it tightly in her hands and tried to strangle it. Then a police car came cruising down the otherwise deserted road. It pulled up alongside us and a policeman poked his head out of the window. For long seconds he stared at the cat curled up around Dayle's head.

"Everything alreet?" he finally asked.

"Yes, yes," I said, "We're just taking a brisk, early-morning walk."

"Wi'a cat?"

"Oh, Merlina *loves* to come along for a spot of exercise."

In the background, Mom's threats to the broomstick became louder and louder. "Drat!" she finally exclaimed, throwing the exhausted broomstick down on the ground, "The stupid thing refuses to obey."

"What won't obey?" asked the policeman.

"Nothing," I told him, smiling. "She's a bit weird, that's all. Likes to sweep the road as she walks, to make sure it's clean, so her shoes don't get dirty."

The policeman scratched his head and looked puzzled. Mom waved her fist at the sleeping broom and swore she would use it as firewood if it didn't get its sticks together fast.

"Ya sure you're alreet?" he asked me.

"Really, we're fine, absolutely fine."

"No, we most certainly are not!" Mom cried, stepping forward. "We are stuck in the middle of nowhere with no *reliable* transport." She threw the broom a vicious stare, then turned back to the policeman and rasped, "I want you to arrest that broom immediately."

The policeman began to clamber out of the car, and I panicked. "If you could just tell us how to get to the Grampian Mountains?" I blurted.

The policeman walked over to where Dayle was perched on a rock with Merlina hissing on her head. "What's the matter with this girl?" he asked.

"Nothing," I beamed brightly, dragging Dayle up onto her feet. "She's just tired, that's all. Aren't you, Dayle?"

Dayle nodded, shook her head, then nodded again. The movement irritated Merlina, who jumped off her head, clawed her way up the front of the policeman's uniform and sky-dived off his shoulder into Mom's arms.

"I nearly fell off," Dayle breathed dreamily. "I was high up in the sky, and I nearly fell off."

"Fell off what?" asked the policeman.

"Off the broomstick."

"The broomstick?"

"She's tired," I said quickly. "Hasn't been feeling too well lately. Keeps imaging all sorts of strange things."

"Should she be out walking this early in the morning if she's not feeling well?" he asked. "Perhaps I can give you all a lift somewhere."

"No, that's okay, thanks all the same."

Mom grew impatient with the small talk. "Look," she said to the policeman, "I'm sure you must have better things to do than stand at the roadside talking to three perfectly happy people. Just give us directions to the Grampian Mountains, and we'll be on our way."

"They're about 120 miles that way," the policeman said, nodding to his left.

"How will we know when we're there?" I asked.

"They're mountains," he laughed, "Big and spikey. You can't possibly miss them."

"I wouldn't be so sure," I muttered, mostly to myself. "Mom could miss Mount Everest unless it had a big red cross painted on the top of it."

"Are you sure we'll be able to spot these apparently unmissable rocks from the air?" Mom asked.

The policeman's mouth fell. His suspicious eyes roamed from Dayle, to me, to Mom. "From the *air*?" he repeated.

"Of course from the air!" Mom snapped. "Do you think we've dragged this broomstick along for the fun of it, useless piece of timber that it is!"

"I think you'd better come along with me to the police station," he said. "There's something not quite right here."

Dayle sighed with heart-felt relief. Merlina hissed. Mom tutted, and I tried to plead our innocence as the policeman lifted the radio attached to the lapel of his jacket and told someone he was bringing in three suspicious characters, a cat, and a broomstick.

I edged Dayle towards the broomstick. I bent down and whispered to it, "If you get us out of her, I'll make sure you get a new coat of varnish as soon as we get home."

The stick leapt up, stood on end, then floated horizontally a metre off the ground. I threw Dayle's leg over the pole and jumped on the back. Mom got on the front, smiled at the policeman, who was frozen to the spot with his mouth wide open and his eyes bulging, and said, "Nice talking to you, officer, but we must be off now, we've a long way to go."

Mom made a big display of checking weather conditions and wind direction with a wet finger, before making the slowest lift-off in the history of witchcraft. She can be a terrible show-off at times. She was lucky the policeman didn't burst into action and pull a few twigs out of the broom's tail as we swooshed passed him, that would have really upset the broomstick.

"Very discreet entry into Scotland, Mom," I drawled sarcastically. "So far we've managed to alert the entire population of Blackpool, a fishing boat, and now a policeman who is probably issuing our descriptions to the whole country at this very moment. Any other plans for our Top Secret mission, Mom?"

"Oh, I thought I might fly around Glasgow for a bit until Fleet Street and the BBC news crews turned up."

"Very funny, Mom. We *are* going the right way this time, aren't we?"

"Of course. Have a bit more faith in your mother. I have a marvellous sense of direction."

But, just to make sure, she asked a passing eagle, "Are we anywhere near the ruins of Dalnaspider Castle?"

The eagle looked not the least bit perturbed that we were flying parallel to him fifty or more metres from the ground. "Och man," it cawed, elegantly flapping its long wings. "Tis reet doon thur b'saide t'loch."

"Pardon me?"

"I thought you had several language degrees, Mom," I laughed, "Including Eskimo, Swahili and Martian."

"I have!" she insisted, "I simply wanted to make sure *you* had understood."

"I understood fine, thanks."

"Good. So what did he say?"

"He said *Och man, tis reet doon thur b'saide t'loch.*"

"Crystal!"

"Okay. Roughly translated he said, 'Well hi there, you gorgeous looking ladies, I'm honoured to tell you that the pleasant abode you seek is right down below by that stretch of water known locally as a loch'."

"That's precisely what I thought he said," Mom said.

We had arrived at last.

CHAPTER SIX

The castle was not exactly a ruin, more of a vague outline of what had once been a castle a very, very long time ago. It had three collapsed walls, and a fourth wall that was merely a jagged path on the ground. Inside this brick box without a lid was a stretch of overgrown grass with a wooden shed in one corner.

"What a dump!" I said, pulling my coat tighter around me as the icy winds blasted down from the surrounding mountains. "How can Dad haunt a castle that's hardly here?"

"Oh, poor Onthe," Mom sobbed. "It's all my fault. If I hadn't nagged at him to come home all the time he'd never have been sent to this awful place as a punishment."

There was no sign of Dad anywhere, which proved he wasn't the best ghost in the world. Far from scaring the living daylights out of unsuspecting visitors, he probably took them on a guided tour around the battlements and nipped down to the local pub regularly for refreshments and a warm-up.

"ONTHE?" Mom called out, "ONTHE, WHERE ARE YOU?"

Dayle suddenly emerged from her coma and started laughing like an insane hyena. "Onthe?" she screamed in disbelief. "Your Dad's name is *Onthe*?"

Mom fixed her with a wicked stare. "And what, might I ask, is wrong with Onthe?"

"Nothing, Mrs *Ball*," Dayle shrieked breathlessly, clutching at her stomach and doubling over. "Nothing at all, Mrs *Ball*." Another peal of hysterical laughter. "Your name wouldn't happen to be Rugby, or Foot, or Passthe, would it, Mrs Ball?"

Mom huffed indignantly. "Certainly not!" she retorted. "My name happens to be Grande."

"Grande Ball!" Dayle howled.

"But her first name is Masq," I said, "Short for Masquerade. My paternal grandfather physically removed three times is called SpotThe, and I have an aunt called Basket."

Dayle obviously couldn't take any more. She wandered off behind a wall to laugh herself to death. I couldn't see what was so funny about our proud family name, and neither could Mom.

"Silly girl," she said. "I've a good mind to make Dayle her second name and Yorkshire her first."

I managed to pull Mom's sparking fingernails down before she had a chance to lob a spell in Dayle's direction.

"Do you think Dad's escaped and gone home?" I asked.

"Possibly." Mom looked around. "But I do sense a presence around here somewhere. It could be your Dad, or it could be psychic vibes from a nearby cemetery, I can't tell."

"DAD?" I screamed. "IT'S ME, CRYSTAL. I"VE COME FOR THE BACK-PAY ON MY POCKET-MONEY."

That was enough to finally bring Dad out into the open. There was nothing he hated more than getting into debt with my pocket money. I charged him interest.

He emerged from behind the far stone wall, dishevelled, bleary-eyed and terribly thin. He normally looks like that, but his hair and clothes looked paler than usual, and his face was more wrinkled than I remembered. He might just have had a bath and not ironed himself out properly, or he might simply be getting old.

My heart heaved as he approached us. When he'd been alive he'd been very handsome, but now he was just a ghost of his former self.

Mom spotted him coming towards us and let out a shriek of delight, flying over like a diving hawk to land in his arms. Unfortunately Mom had forgotten that, because Dad's a ghost, he doesn't have any real arms in which to catch her. Mom went right through his semi-transparent body and landed flat on her face behind him.

"Masquie!" Dad cried, trying to help her up with his wispy white hands, "How wonderful to see you, my love."

Mom struggled awkwardly to her feet and stood before him like a wide-eyed schoolgirl with a crush. "I've missed you so much," she cooed.

"My sweet."

"My petal."

"My angel."

"My, Onthe, how pale you look."

"It's the weather," said Dad. "It's so cold all the time, and you can't get a decent bite to eat around here for love nor money."

"I don't suppose there's much demand for spirit soup or cosmic casserole," I said, eager for him to notice me and give me a hug.

He turned to me and smiled. My Dad's got a great smile. It's very broad. In fact, in stretches all the way from one ear to the other, almost splitting his face in half. He got it from a goblin shop that sold smiles, but he wasn't sure how big his face was and ended up buying one three sizes too big.

"How's my darling Crystal been?" he asked.

"Naughty," said Mom, before I could answer. "She's used baby wishes to send an innocent child into space, and turned her best friend into a piece of paper."

Dad's response came quickly. He opened his mouth wide, and burst out into laughter that echoed and bounced off what remained of the castle walls. He laughed so hard he cracked his face open, and the top half of his head fell back and rested against the back of his neck. His laughter stopped as he struggled to pull it up again.

Mom looked annoyed. "This is no laughing matter, Onthe. I think you should have a serious talk with your daughter."

Dad composed himself. "Of course, my love, my sweet." Then, turning to me, he asked, "What would you like to talk about first, Crystal? Homework? The mysteries of life? How to lose your soul in three easy steps?"

"I mean about this boy!" Mom snapped. "She's deposited him

on some uninhabited planet in the centre of the galaxy."

"Not that horrible boy who's been picking on you and Dayle at school?" Dad asked.

"Yes," I said, "How did you know?"

"Merlina told a neighbouring cat about it, who told a visiting relative, who mentioned it to another cat, who happened to be friendly with the cat who lives in the hotel down the road. From what I've heard," Dad said, "That boy deserved to be blasted into space. How is Dayle, by the way?"

"Oh, fine. She's over there somewhere, laughing her head off, but other than that she's fine."

Dad patted the top of his own head and grinned. "I always knew me and Dayle would find something in common. But you better tell her to be careful if her head falls off, there's a dreadful shortage of heads at the moment and someone might try to run off with it."

Mom furiously crossed her arms over her chest and impatiently began tapping her foot on the turf. "If I could interrupt for just a moment," she said, "Perhaps, Onthe, since you're so amused by Crystal's antics, you could tell us how we're going to bring this poor child back down to earth again?"

Dad put a finger to his chin, stared up at the sky, hummed a bit, then shrugged. "Haven't a clue," he said.

A huge cloud of disappointment fell over me. Dads were supposed to know everything, have the answer to every problem. We'd come all this way for nothing. And Haig was running out of time, I could sense it.

"But we can ask Ollie for advice, if you like?" Dad said.

"Who's Ollie?"

"My mate. Come on, I'll introduce you."

Dad guided us to a flight of stairs that were obscured behind the wooden hut in the corner of the castle grounds. The worn steps took us down to a long corridor, which must have once been part of the dungeons.

"Spooky," I whispered into the darkness, as we felt our way along the damp walls.

"If you think this is spooky," Dad said, "Wait until you meet some of the inhabitants around here."

I could hardly wait.

The corridor eventually opened up into a small claustrophobic cellar that was lit by a single candle. Chains and other nasty devices hung from the rocky ceiling, and the remains of a medieval rack stood pride of place in the centre. Over by the far wall was a shadowy fire that Dad was cooking two ghostly fish on. The fish lay side by side on a flat piece of tin metal, calmly discussing the weather.

"So, where's this Ollie fellow?" Mom asked.

"*Who*?"

"Ollie. The friend you said might be able to help us."

"*Who*?"

"That's him," said Dad, pointing up at a stick that was jutting out of the wall and which had a large brown bird perched upon it. "Ollie the owl."

"Pleased to meet you, Ollie," I said.

"Likewise," said the owl, "Though I must point out that my real name is Sir Olivier Lawrence De Whit, the third in a long line of notorious De Whits that once flew free over the wild moors of the Highlands when Scotland was - "

"He rambles on a bit," Dad whispered. "You have to grab his attention firmly with both hands to make him stop blabbering. OI, OLLIE!" he yelled, "WE'D LIKE TO TALK TO YOU."

"No need to yell at me, Onthe," said Ollie. "I may be dead, but I'm certainly not deaf."

"Ollie's a ghost, too?" I gasped.

"Recently departed," Dad whispered. "Very nasty accident with a farmer and a shotgun, but he doesn't like to talk about it much."

Dad told Ollie about our problem with Haig. Ollie was so fascinated with the story he buried his head under his wing and promptly fell asleep.

"He's thinking about it," Dad said.

"He's *asleep*," said Mom.

"He thinks better when he's asleep."

"He's not going to help us, is he, Dad?"

Dad tried to pat me on the shoulder, but his hand went straight through me and made my bones tingle. "Ollie will come up with something, I'm sure he will. We'll just have to wait until he wakes up again."

We settled down on some smooth rocks around the ghostly fire to await Ollie's final verdict. The family get-together might have been quite cosy, except that ghostly fires aren't real fires and don't give off any real heat. With my clothes damp from the sea-storm and my bones cold from the icy winds that had blasted through me on the journey, I was frozen. I didn't want to complain, so I sat next to my Dad, shivering a great deal and trying to stop my teeth from chattering too loudly.

"So, how have you been?" Mom asked Dad.

"Not too bad."

"Have you been lonely without me, my sweet?"

"No, not really." Mom's face fell, but Dad didn't seem to notice her heartbroken expression. "There's so many interesting characters wandering around this castle," he said, "I haven't had a chance to feel lonely."

"What characters, Onthe?" Mom pouted.

"There's Ben, he's a soldier who got killed in a war right outside these very walls. Had his head chopped off and a six foot lance stuck in him."

"Lovely," Mom said, "A headless soldier on a stick."

"Then there's Donald," Dad continued. "He claims to be a Scottish king. And Rupert, who died of food poisoning. Ethelred contracted a rather nasty disease of the liver, John was crushed by falling masonry, and - "

"Where are they now?" I asked, excited to meet them all.

"They're out gallivanting in the nearby town, no doubt chasing all the women."

"But you don't do that sort of thing, do you, Onthe?" Mom said.

"No, dearest. I stay behind to keep Janine company."

"Janine!" Mom spat. "Who's Janine?"

Dad looked flustered, confused, uncertain what to say next. "No-one, my pet, my angel," he smiled. "She's just a poor orphan spook who wanders around the castle walls moaning and rattling her chains a lot."

"Is she young?" Mom hissed.

"Yes, as a matter of fact she - "

"Is she *pretty*?" Mom's eyes were glowing bright green in the dark.

"Er, yes, a bit."

"I see!" Mom threw herself down across the floor to have a good sulk. Dad stared at her, not knowing what he'd done or said to upset her.

"How come the Chief Magician sent you here to haunt when it's already overrun with ghosts?" I asked, to break the tension.

"They're old ghosts," Dad said, still frowning down at Mom. "They've been here so long the mortals have grown used to them. The Chief Magician hoped I would stir up a bit of enthusiasm amongst the tourists. The local people earn a good living from the castle's haunted reputation, selling stuffed ghosts and headless dolls. When trade dropped off they insisted that the Chief Magician supply them with some new ghosts because the old ones were so boring."

"They don't sound boring to me."

"No, well you haven't had to live with them for the last two hundred years, so the old ghosts are new ghosts to you."

"Ooooh," interrupted a voice. "Ooooh. I dooo believe I know how to solve the little problem you have with the boy on another planet."

We all jumped up and rushed expectantly over to Ollie's perch. Ollie, pleased with such an undivided show of attention, ruffled his wing feathers and spent a long time coughing a non-existent frog out of his throat before speaking.

"It once happened to a cousin of mine," he began, "One Clarence Vanderbilt De Whit, back in the seventeenth century. I understand he committed some petty crime involving a certain female owl of the Barn persuasion, and the entire De Whit family sent him to Coventry as a punishment for his appallingly bad taste in owls. I can't rightly recall how they managed to bring him back again, but if it comes to mind, I'll be sure to let you know."

"You've been a big help," Mom said, rolling her eyes.

"Anytime," Ollie said, and he went back to sleep.

A noise filtered down into the dungeon just then, a scream that was instantly recognisable as Dayle's from the incredibly high-pitched tone and the familiar quaver of terror. I ran to the entrance of the cellar, just as she raced down the dark corridor. We collided, and she let out another blood-curdling scream.

"What is it?" I asked, "What's the matter?"

Dayle couldn't speak, she just kept on screaming. Dad came up and stood towering over her as she jumped from one foot to the other, shaking her hands out in front of her like they were on fire. When Dayle turned her head and saw my Dad's deathly pallor, she screamed even louder.

"I do wish that child would stop doing that," Mom muttered in the background.

"For heaven's sake, Dayle," I said, "Get a grip on yourself."

She took a firm grip of my damp coat instead, and with her eyeballs still riveted to my Dad's wavering apparition, she shrieked, "I've just seen a ghost."

"That's no ghost," I told her. "That's my Dad."

"No!" she cried, pushing me backwards and forwards with her clenched fists, "Not that one. There's another one. Outside."

"What did it look like?"

"It looked like a ghost, what do you think it looked like?"

"Describe it."

Dayle shuddered. "It was *horrible*, all bloody and wailing, with a spear sticking out of its body. It pulled the stick out and started picking its teeth with it. Then it took its head off and began bouncing it on the ground like a basketball player."

"That's Ben," Dad said. "If you ask him real nice he'll let you play pass-kick with him."

"I don't want to play pass-kick!" Dayle screamed. "Please,

don't make me play with its head."

"It's okay, Dayle," I said, patting the back of her head when she threw it onto my shoulder and began to cry. I looked up at Dad. "Do you think any of your other friends will be able to help us sort Haig out?"

"I doubt it," Dad said. "Ben lost his brains ages ago during a friendly football match with the spooks over at Glenco. We searched the pitch for ages afterwards but we never found them. John's brains got squashed when a ton of rock fell on his head, and the others never really had any to begin with."

"What about *Janine*?" Mom said, making the name sound like a contagious disease. "I bet she's clever as well as *beautiful*"

"I don't want to bother her with our little problem," Dad replied. "She's very sensitive, very delicate, and she gets upset easily."

"Poor thing," Mom said coldly. "Pack your bags, Onthe, we're leaving."

"Leaving? But why?"

"Because I'm not letting you stay here with some pretty, clever, sensitive little girl a second longer."

Dad broke into one of his enormous smiles again. "Masquie," he breathed, "You're jealous!"

"I am not. Yes I am."

"Oh Masquie, that's so sweet." Dad placed a ghostly kiss on her cheek. "But, my love, my angel cake with icing on the top, I can't leave. The Chief Magician will notice my absence, and who knows where he'll send me next time."

Mom started to cry. She tried to rest her tear-stained face on Dad's shoulder, but fell through it instead. Dayle, who had now calmed down to a nervous state of terror, whispered something about wishing she'd never got mixed up with such a seriously weird family.

"Don't they ever … you know, *kiss*, or anything?" she asked me.

"All the time."

"How do they … you know, do it?"

"When they want to participate in a bit of sloppy stuff, Mom turns herself into a spirit. Only she's too upset to do it at the moment."

"Silly me," Dayle said. "I should have guessed it would be something as simple and straightforward as that."

"We need you, Onthe," Mom was saying. "We need you at home, to help us, look after us, so things like this don't happen."

"But I can't leave the castle, Masquie. I'll get into worse trouble than I'm in already."

Mom considered this for a long moment. Then her eyes lit up and she said, "We can draw you in the magic book. We'll just sketch another ghost and leave that one here to take your place so that you can come home with us."

"But if we do that, then I'll only have one wish left," I cried.

My parents were too busy dancing and skipping around in delight, celebrating Mom's cleverness, to listen to me. Dayle looked at me flatly and drawled, "We didn't bring the drawing book with us, did we. How can we draw another ghost if we don't have the book?"

"No problem," Mom said, and she waved her long fingernails in the air until bright sparkles flashed across the rocky ceiling. There was a flash and a cough, a tinkle and a sneeze, and then the book appeared on the rock by the fire. The fish jumped up to have a look, and knocked it into the flames. Dad rushed over to retrieve it. When he pulled it from the ghostly flames his arm was on fire. He stood staring at it, smiling and frowning at the same time. Mom had to use one of the fish to put his arm out. The fish wasn't too happy about it.

In the now slightly scorched book, I quickly drew a picture of a ghost with a big, big smile. We all held our breath as I touched one of the bright stars on the cover, and sighed with relief when a paper-thin caricature of my Dad materialised before our eyes.

"Do you think it will fool the Chief Magician?" I asked, worried that our paper ghost looked much too much like a paper ghost.

"As long as he can sense someone who looks like me is

wandering around the castle," Dad said, "I don't think he'll bother taking a closer look."

Dad gave his paper twin detailed instructions about haunting. The thin twin flapped its head in response and smiled broadly, before floating flimsily down the corridor to start its duties.

"Can we go home now?" Dayle asked.

"Sure."

Outside, we found Merlina mercilessly teasing a couple of black rats with her sharp claws. She claimed they'd been gnawing on the broomstick and she was simply trying to scare them off, but the rats insisted they were innocent and wouldn't dare touch a witch's broomstick. Mom gave them the benefit of the doubt and threatened to turn Merlina into a goldfish if she didn't behave herself.

Mom summoned the broom. It stayed firmly rooted to the ground. I whispered the word, "Varnish," and it suddenly sprang to life. We all clambered aboard, Dayle muttering about the joys of normal transport and Dad complaining that he had to share the uncomfortable brush end with Merlina, who was taking up more than her fair share of the space.

"Oi, Onthe, old mate," came a crackly voice.

A soldier with a long pole sticking out of his chest appeared from behind the castle wall. He had his head under one arm, and under the other arm he held a young girl from the local village who was giggling madly.

"Ben," Dad shouted across to him, "I'm off to solve a domestic crisis at home. Cover for me, will you?"

"What shall I tell Janine? She'll be upset if you don't say goodbye."

Dad avoided Mom's bulging green eyes. "Tell her goodbye for me. And don't keep tossing your head into her lap to get her attention because she doesn't like it. And don't - "

"Can we *go*?" Mom snapped.

Dad nodded, waved at Ben, and shouted, "I'll be back as soon as I can."

Mom took off, muttering that she'd rather have him exorcised than let him return to this place.

The broomstick wasn't very happy about all the extra weight it was expected to carry, despite the fact that Dad was a ghost and didn't weigh anything at all. It did a loop-the-loop in the air, then spun round and round until Mom clobbered it one. It sulked for the rest of the journey.

Mom flew a bit close to Manchester airport and nearly collided with a Boeing 747, which was filled with shocked holiday makers who peered out of the round windows and took photos of us. Mom quickly brought out a lipstick and asked us if her hair looked alright, and then posed for the cameras.

We then disrupted a flock of geese flying south for the winter. The broomstick was so shocked by their honking noise it skidded to a sudden halt in mid-air, and Merlina fell off. It took ages for us to locate her, clinging precariously to the top-most branch of a pine tree. Merlina then joined in the big sulk with the broomstick, while Dayle cried and Mom and Dad argued about a certain young ghost. On the whole, it wasn't a particularly good trip home.

Cuthbert was delighted to see us back again. He licked the air where Dad's body should have been, if he'd had one, and even gave Merlina a huge slobber of welcome. She hissed at him and skulked off to clean the pine needles out of her fur.

"It's good to be home." Dad sighed, smiling as he wandered around the kitchen, giving the cooker, the fridge and the sink taps a friendly pat.

"It's nice to have you back, Dad," I said.

It felt like we were a real family again. Even Mom forgot that she was angry with him and smiled. They came together across the crowded room with their eyes full of gooeyness, and it was obvious they were about to start snogging – yuk.

"I must go," Dayle coughed awkwardly, as Mom began to turn into a spirit. "I'll speak to you soon, Crystal," she said, racing down the hallway to the front door, "Or maybe I won't, I haven't decided yet, but I'll be sure to let you know if we're still friends or not as soon as - "

She stopped in mid-sentence. I popped my head around the kitchen door to make sure she was alright, and saw her standing rigid in front of the open door. Maybe she'd forgotten something, I thought.

Then Dayle turned round. Her eyes were like pickled onions. I'd never seen her look so scared.

And then I saw why. When Dayle stepped slightly to one side, I had a clear view of someone standing on our doorstep. Someone very tall and imposing, with a long white beard and a long black robe. Someone who had an air of supreme authority about him, and who was wearing an expression of explosive anger.

It was the Chief Magician.

CHAPTER SEVEN

I just had time to give a quick warning to Mom and Dad, before that heavy black cloak came billowing into our house.

Dayle took one look at this enormous stranger with the long white beard and pointed hat, and darted out of the front door. I envied her. With Dad home when he shouldn't be and me in big trouble about Haig, I would have liked to have run off too. The wrath of the Chief Magician was not to be taken lightly. I could easily be sent to the Witches Rehabilitation Centre for Rebellious Teenagers, and Dad could be transported to the Lost Souls Department.

"Hide, *quick!*" I hissed.

Mom was in the middle of changing into a spirit so that she could suck lips with Dad, but when she heard the urgency in my voice she quickly reverted back to her normal form. Grabbing Dad by the neck, she stuffed him into a teapot.

The Chief Magician swept into the kitchen. His face was like a stormy sky about to erupt, and his eyes flashed like lightning. Mom immediately started acting like the busy housewife she wasn't, putting the teapot in the breadbin, and then putting the breadbin in the cupboard under the sink. There wasn't even the slightest waver in her voice as she greeted the Magician with a most charming smile, and said, "Why, Chiefy, what an unexpected but extremely pleasant surprise."

The Chief Magician said nothing in reply. He dismissed my presence with dark look, and I staggered back to sit at the end of the table, as far away from him as I could get.

"What brings you to our humble abode?" Mom asked, "Of course you're welcome in our home at *any* time, day or night."

I noticed that the edges of her mouth were beginning to twitch with nerves and prayed the magician wouldn't spot the way her hands were shaking like dry leaves in a breeze.

The Magician's voice, when it finally came, was deep and hard and crusty. "There is," he boomed like a foghorn, "a most disturbing atmosphere coming from this house." Several teacups and three crystal glasses had vibrated off a shelf and toppled to the floor with a crash by the time he'd finished speaking.

I tried to slither underneath the table and disappear. Mom remained impressively calm, steadying her trembling legs against the sink cupboard. "Chiefy, darling," she cooed, puckering up her lips and fluttering her eyelashes a great deal, "Are you sure it's *this* house that is the cause of all those vibes? I mean, there's a really cosmic-disturbing family living just a few doors down the road."

"*This* house," he insisted, flapping his arms around in agitation and knocking a few decorative plates off the wall with his long sleeves.

Mom shrugged nonchalantly. "What sort of aural disturbances are we talking about here, Chiefy?"

"Aural disturbances of the *bad* kind," he said, eyes flashing. "I've been picking up unusual brain patterns from one of you, something about a missing person, gross abuse of magic powers, and a blatant disregard for the Solemn Oath of Secrecy."

"Pardon?" Mom said.

The Magician glared at her. She glared back, not blinking, hardly breathing. A tense, heavy silence filled the room. Neither of them noticed Cuthbert, in desperate need of a hug from my Dad, pawing at the sink cupboard.

"I've had to have words with you about wasting magic power before, haven't I, Grande Ball?"

"Yes, but that was only for minor face changes, domestic chores and little things like that. Nothing big. I don't know what all the fuss was about in the first place."

As she spoke, she gently tried to push Cuthbert away from

the cupboard with her toe of her foot, but Cuthbert was having none of it. He hadn't seen his master in a long time and he was determined to get to him now, despite Mom trying to put the boot in.

The Chief Magician stared intensely at Mom, searching her face for any signs of deception. Mom smiled innocently and kicked Cuthbert so hard he gambolled across the floor and let out an exaggerated cry of pain.

"What *is* the matter with that dog?" the Magician demanded to know.

Cuthbert darted back to the cupboard and started whimpering.

"He's hungry," Mom said. "We keep his food in there."

"Indeed."

The Chief Magician turned to me. I cringed back in my chair. His eyes were so dark they looked like shiny lumps of coal embedded in his wrinkled face. His nose was long and straight, and he had a matted white beard that almost touched the floor and which seemed to have something living inside of it. I couldn't distinguish between his wild eyebrows and his hairline, and he was so tall his pointed hat was crumpled up against the ceiling. He was certainly an awesome, fearful person to have standing in our kitchen.

"You!" he roared, pointing a knobbled finger in my direction, "Have you been doing anything you shouldn't have been doing?"

"Me, Sir? No, Sir. Absolutely not, Sir. Never. Sir."

He huffed furiously, buried his fingers in his beard and had a good scratch. Casting suspicious eyes around the room, he groaned so loudly it sounded like a volcano about to explode. "I'll get to the bottom of this sooner or later," he promised.

And, with that, he spun round, knocked a saucepan stand over with his billowing cloak, and stormed off down the hallway.

"Always a pleasure to see you," Mom called after him, grabbing Cuthbert firmly by the collar and shaking him, "Do come again soon, you'll be more than welcome."

The front door slammed shut and he was gone.

Dad was retrieved from the teapot in the breadbin in the cupboard. He looked whiter than he normally looked.

"He's onto us," he said. "He knows we're up to something. Have you ever seen him in such a temper?" Mom and I both shook our heads. "Not many people have witnessed his wrath and lived. If he finds out I'm here he'll … Oh dear," he began to wail, "Oh dear, oh dear."

"Don't you worry about a thing, my love," Mom soothed. "We'll sort out the business with Haig, then you'll get straight back to that castle before he's even noticed you're missing." Then, obviously remembering about Janine, the pretty ghost, she quickly added, "Or perhaps we'll find a way to get you transferred to a castle a bit closer to home, where I can keep an eye on you."

It took a strong cup of ectoplasm tea before Dad managed to stop quaking in his ghostly boots. When he finally got his brain-cells back in order, he turned to me and said, "I have to visit the scene of the crime, get a taste of the atmosphere where the event took place, before I can figure out how to bring Haig back."

I stopped breathing. My heart stopped beating. "But … it happened at school, Dad. I can't take you to the school. We're not even allowed to bring pets into the classroom."

"It has to be done, Crystal. It's the only way."

Which is why, the following morning, I walked tentatively to school with Dad neatly folded up inside my satchel. Dayle was taking the day off to recover from the previous night, so I had no-one to give me support or courage.

When I entered my form class I had butterflies the size of vultures crashing around in my stomach. I wasn't quite sure what Dad was going to do, and he wouldn't tell me, which only made me feel more nervous.

My first lesson was History, and that was okay. Dad remained in my satchel on the floor and only occasionally poked his head out to have a look around. Mabel Riley, who sat at the desk behind mine, did suddenly slump in a dead faint across her desk after leaning down to pick a pencil up off the floor but, apart from that, no-one else noticed I had brought my Dad to school.

Until Geography. Mr Jewit was rambling on about contour lines and mountain ranges, and Dad started to get restless, as we all did. My satchel tipped over quite a few times for no apparent reason. It was only when my satchel began to slide across the floor and wriggle about underneath Martin Bell's desk did people start to suspect something.

Mr Jewit made me take the offending bag outside if it was going to cause so much disruption. I actually rushed it down to the gym and stuffed Dad into a changing room locker.

"Now you stay there and behave yourself," I hissed at him, just as a gym teacher walked passed and stared at me oddly. When the gym teacher had gone, I whispered, "I'll come back for you at break time and show you where it happened."

But since when has my Dad ever taken any notice of me?

I was having a peaceful doze in English lesson, with Miss Simpson raving on and on about Romeo again, when the class door squeaked open. Curious, everyone raised their heads off their desks to watch the visitor enter the room.

Only there was no-one there. The door eerily closed shut again. It was just the wind blowing through the window John Busk had broken with a hockey ball last summer, everyone thought, and started to go back to sleep.

Then there came the clear sound of footsteps plodding across the classroom floor. *Thud, shuffle, thud, shuffle.* Eyes grew wide, and Miss Simpson clutched Shakespeare's book tight to her chest.

The footsteps went passed Virginia Crane, *thud, shuffle, thud, shuffle,* passed William Goldberg, *thud, shuffle, thud, shuffle,* and down the aisle by the window, *thud, shuffle, thud, shuffle.*

They stopped abruptly at my desk, and I felt an invisible hand tap my shoulder.

"I'm bored," came an spooky voice.

Thirty-two children and a very hysterical teacher vacated the classroom within seconds. I was *so* embarrassed.

"Dad!" I cried, "I told you to stay in the locker."

"It was cold," he said, "And claustrophobic. And someone had left a smelly football sock in there, I almost suffocated."

I stuffed him back into my satchel and took him with me to the Biology lesson. It was there that the *real* trouble started. Dad kept trying to wriggle out of my bag and I kept having to push his head back in again. During one particularly sensitive experiment, when the whole class was gathered around a table waiting for a chemical to change colour, Dad began to whine.

"Lemme out," he wailed. "I'm uncomfortable. It's stuffy in here. And what on earth are you doing carrying a sharp protractor around without a protective cover?"

"What's that noise?" the teacher asked.

"It's my radio," I said. "It must have turned itself on."

"Well turn it back off again, Crystal Ball, and hurry up about it."

I ran to the satchel on my desk, clobbered it, hissed for him to keep his oversized mouth shut, and went back to the restless group around the experiment bench.

"May we now continue?" the teacher asked me.

"Sure, go right ahead."

"You only got five out of ten in the Maths exam!" exclaimed a voice. "I thought you said you were doing well in Maths? And why do your book covers have dirty footprints all over them, Crystal?"

I smiled. I shrank. I shuffled back towards my satchel with twenty-nine impatient, curious, amused faces watching my every move.

"Silly radio," I giggled nervously.

I took my satchel off my desk, dropped it to the floor and kicked it under the locust tank.

"Ouch!" it cried, "That hurt. You don't have to be so *rough*, you know."

"*Then be quiet!*"

The class started laughing at my antics with an apparently live satchel that answered back. Mr Wallis was so annoyed with me for disturbing his experiment his eyebrows knitted together and red veins stood out on his neck.

"Will you *please* stop that infernal racket and join the rest of the class," he growled.

"Yes, sir."

The experiment was, by now, ruined because of the delay. Mr Wallis huffed, scowled, then bent down to grab something from beneath his bench. He brought up a metal tray that had a little green frog stretched out on it. Some girls screwed up their faces at the sight, but all the boys looked eager as Mr Wallis attached electrodes to the dead creature.

"Since our first experiment was disrupted," he said, glaring at me, "We'll go straight onto the next; What happens when you introduce an electric current through a dead body?"

"Dead body!" Dad cried. "You're going to run an electric current through a *dead body*! Crystal, that might easily have been your great aunt in a previous existence."

The flap of my satchel flew open and Dad blasted into the classroom like a shredded white sheet. He shot over the empty desks to where Mr Wallis was standing by the experiment bench surrounded by wide-eyed pupils. Mr Wallis didn't look annoyed or angry now, he looked like quivering custard.

Dad floated down beside him and reached out a ghostly hand to stroke the dead frog on the metal tray. "It's okay, Auntie," he said, "I'll save you." Then, turning to Mr Wallis, he snarled, "This shouldn't be allowed in front of children. We never had this kind of practice when *I* was at school."

"When was that?" some brave child dared to ask this ghost in its midst.

For a moment Dad was silent in thought, and then he replied, "In the fifteenth century, I think. Or was that the lifetime before? I can't remember. A very long time ago, anyway."

During this casual conversation, Mr Wallis had time to get his composure back. He threw back his shoulders, puffed out his chest, and faced up to his unwelcome intruder.

"Experimenting on frogs is part of the national curriculum," he said.

"The what?" said Dad.

"It's educational policy to demonstrate to children how a body, even a dead one, reacts when an electric current is passed through it. We were also, before you so *rudely* interrupted us, about to examine this frog's brain tissue to discover if - "

"Hey," Dad grinned, "If you want to examine brain tissue, take a look at *this*."

And before I could stop him, Dad had flipped the top of his head back to reveal the mouldy brain embedded in the top of his skull.

The sight was too much for my fellow pupils and, with much screaming and pushing, they left the classroom in a disorderly fashion.

"Call the Ghostbusters!" somebody yelled down the corridor.

Only Mr Wallis remained, and he was pinned flat against the blackboard, totally unable to tear his eyes off Dad's exposed brain. Dad plucked out the soggy grey matter and thumped it down on the bench top. It smelt awful.

"There," he said, "Examine *that*."

"Dad," I said, "I don't think a decomposed brain will be of much use to anyone."

Dad shrugged, picked his brain up, and pushed it back inside his skull with a wet squelch. Then he snapped his head shut again. Mr Wallis rolled his eyes to the heavens, slithered down the blackboard, and fell into an untidy heap on the floor.

"Poor man's tired," Dad said, "He's obviously been working too hard." Then, turning back to the little green frog on the metal tray, he said, "Make it better again, Crystal."

"What?"

"Make it better."

"But Dad, it's *dead*."

"So?"

So? So what? Most of my relatives were dead, but that doesn't stop them from visiting us every Christmas, disrupting the neighbourhood and smothering me in slimy kisses. But this was a *frog*, not a relative, and Dad wasn't asking me to kiss it or pull a cracker with it or anything simple like that. He was asking me to bring it back to life again.

"I'm not allowed to use magic spells until I'm sixteen," I

reminded him.

"Then use the book."

"The book?"

"The magic book of children's wishes. Draw a picture of it looking happy with its family, in a big pond full of lilies."

I couldn't believe what he was asking me to do. "But it's my last wish, Dad." And I wasn't about to waste it on some little green frog.

"One frog, one wish," Dad smiled. "What's the problem?"

"But ... but ... I haven't wished for Bloodthorn Thunderbluster Maze III to fall madly in love with me yet."

Dad straightened himself up and began to glow with temper, like a light bulb going on and off. "Crystal Ball!" he said. "I didn't teach you to be so selfish, and I don't think you deserve to keep the last wish all to yourself when this poor little frog needs your help."

He was starting to sound like a real Dad, stern and unreasonable.

"But Dad - "

"No buts, Crystal. I think the life of this little green frog is infinitely more important than making some teenager girl's crush come true - "

"But it's *Bloodthorn Thunderbluster Maze III*, Dad," I said in hushed tones of reverence, "The most gorgeous wizard on the face of the planet."

"I don't care if they're kings of England, I want to see this frog reunited with its family. Its tadpoles are probably crying for it at this very minute. Now do it."

So I did it, reluctantly, slowly, all the time thinking of Bloodthorn running off with someone else because he'd never had the chance to meet me, the girl of their dreams. I wanted to cry.

I snatched the book out of my satchel, opened it up with a huff, and quickly scribbled a rough scene. A little pond filled with happy, croaking frogs and lush vegetation growing all around it. A frog paradise. I pouted miserably at Dad as I closed the cover and touched the last, the very last, bright star.

And there it was, a frog jumping up off the metal tray,

looking so glad to be alive. And there was the lily pond full of tadpoles and frogs all croaking out for it to join them. Locusts, hamsters, gerbils and the rabid guinea pig scrabbled out of their cages to feast on the lush vegetation and live happily ever after. It was a pleasant scene, a happy scene, a scene to warm the very arteries of the heart.

Right in the middle of the Biology class.

"There you are," said Dad. "The school's very own nature reserve, all under one roof. They won't have to worry about studying the wildlife in bad weather now."

A blue tit flew in through the open window and settled in an oak tree that had suddenly grown by the teacher's desk. Three baby blackbirds and their mother followed, as did a group of swifts, a family of sparrows, and about three million starlings. The noise drowned out the sound of slushy Walt Disney music playing in the background.

"I think we'd better get out of here," I said, grabbing hold of Dad's arm and making a bolt for the door.

Water poured out of the pond, ran like a river down the corridor and cascaded like a waterfall down three flights of stairs into the hallway below. A lone tadpole got caught in the current and hung onto a banister rail for dear life, until its mother hopped along to rescue it.

In our haste to escape before we were caught, we ran straight into a class emerging from the Physics laboratory. They took one look at Dad, floating in mid air with his ragged clothes ruffling in a ghostly breeze, and went completely bonkers. Pandemonium was the order of the day. The sound of gushing water and multiple screaming echoed around the school.

The children in the adjoining Chemistry class came out to see what all the noise was about. They saw the scattering of shrieking bodies splashing down the corridor, then noticed Dad hovering above their heads with a stupid grin on his face. Their screams added to the general chaos.

Suddenly, the corridor was filled with frantic pupils in soggy uniforms feverishly wading to safety. They slipped down the stairs and disrupted all the classes peacefully dozing through an English lesson on the floor below.

All of this alarm alarmed Dad. He didn't like to see children upset, and he started to cry. His cry came out as a wailing sound, which alarmed the pupils even more, which made Dad howl louder, which made the pupils ...

Meanwhile, the headmaster had turned up to investigate. Far from taking control of the situation, he saw my Dad hovering near the ceiling, turned on his heels and pushed children out of the way as he ran back to his office.

The Physics teacher fainted. The Chemistry teacher called for someone to phone for the Ghostbusters.

"We've called, they're busy," a child called back, "But we found a ghost hunter on Google who lives quite close and we're trying to negotiate a price."

"A ghost hunter!" Dad shrieked. "That's it! I'm out of here."

"Good idea, Dad."

I thought we would have to fight our way through the crowds as mass hysteria broke out all over school. But, upon sight of Dad, still floating in mid air and glowing like a hundred watt light bulb, everyone politely cleared a path for us.

We raced down to the ground floor and found three muscled gym teachers standing shoulder to shoulder at the bottom of the stairs waiting for us. They looked ready and eager for a fight, a battle to the death with a wandering ghost.

"Quick, over the banister," I yelled at Dad.

He floated over the side of the staircase and into a cupboard. The gym teachers chased after him, one clutching a hockey stick, one wielding a cricket bat, and the other wearing boxing gloves. I leapt down the stairs, ran across the foyer outside the main assembly hall, and through the doors into the fresh air.

Dad, terrified he was being abandoned by his only child, blasted out of the cupboard. The force of the door flying open sent the three gym teachers reeling backwards in three different directions. Dad blew across the foyer like a whirlwind and dived straight into the satchel he claimed he hated so much.

The gym teachers staggered to their feet, their square faces twisted in pain and their eyes blazing in anger. I sprinted passed the ground level classrooms to the back of the school, where the dustbins were lined up outside the kitchens like a row of fat metal soldiers. I stuffed my satchel into the nearest bin, just as the gym teachers rounded the corner.

"He's gone," I told them.

"Gone where?" they growled.

"Gone home."

The teachers weren't convinced and started searching the area. I gingerly backed away, not wanting to hang around in case they got suspicious, but not wanting to leave Dad either.

I waited by the side entrance gates for ages until the teachers finally gave up and wandered back into school muttering furiously amongst themselves. I retrieved my satchel from the dustbin, but Dad wasn't in it. He'd gone again.

"DAD!" I yelled. "DAD!"

"Crystal," came a voice from above. I looked up. Dad was floating outside a second floor classroom window.

Suddenly his voice was smothered by the screaming of terrified children who had spotted him. Even from the ground outside I could hear the sounds of toppled furniture as a whole classroom made a mad dash for the door.

"Crystal," Dad called, "Is this the classroom where it happened?"

"Yes," I yelled back.

Dad floated through the window. There was a single cry of horror from some child who hadn't left with everyone else, who was probably hiding under a desk. I heard the desk topple over, and the single cry quickly faded into the distance.

Dad eventually reappeared in the air above my head and floated down next to me.

"Have you figured out how to bring Haig back?" I asked anxiously.

Dad shook his head. "There's too much interference," he said. "I can't concentrate with all this noise going on. The only vibes I can pick up are of a little boy flicking paperclips at a little girl, and a male member of staff trying to kiss a female member of staff in the stock cupboard."

"Really?" I gasped, fascinated, "Which members of staff?"

Dad gave me vague descriptions of what could have been half the teachers in school. As I was pressing him for more information, Dayle mysteriously turned up, galloping up the school driveway as if she had the hounds of hell chasing after her.

"I thought you were in bed resting after yesterday's adventures?" I said.

Dayle didn't answer. Her face was flushed red and she was panting like a hot dog. Leaning with one hand against the school wall, she gasped for breath and tried to speak. "Haig," she spluttered. "I know ... I know how we can bring Haig back."

"You do?"

CHAPTER EIGHT

Dayle's idea was a good one, the best we'd come up with so far. And Dad agreed it was probably the only chance we had of ever bringing Haig back to earth again.

There was just one slight problem, one tiny hitch in the plan that nobody had considered. I tried to get a word in edgeways as we walked home from school to tell Mom, but Dad and Dayle were too busy discussing details in excited little voices to listen to me.

"It won't work," I kept saying, shaking my head as I opened the front door. "It ... won't ... work."

"Of course it will work," Dayle said. "Somebody should have thought of it before."

"Yes," I agreed, "Somebody *should* have done."

"Come on, girls," Dad said, as Mom came out of the kitchen and into the living room to see what was happening, "Let's not argue and fall out, not at a time like this. We should at least try it, Crystal. What have we got to lose?"

"What's happening?" Mom asked.

Cuthbert and Merlina, sensing the build-up of excitement in the house, came padding down the stairs.

"Dayle has come up with a brilliant plan to bring Haig back," Dad said.

"Oh thank goodness," Mom sighed, "Well done, Dayle. Very well done indeed."

We all sat in the living room, the blotchy, multi-coloured living room. Mom and Dad sat huddled together on the sofa, I collapsed into a chair with Dayle perched on the arm.

"So, what's the plan then?" Mom asked, when the silence dragged on too long.

"Well," Dayle said, enjoying the attention as everyone held their breath to listen to every word she uttered. "I was lying in bed this morning when the answer suddenly came to me. I heard my mother downstairs, shouting at my little brother, Thomas. He'd pushed a bowl of porridge off his high-chair table and my mother was moaning about having to make some more. Do you get it?" she asked, eyes wide. "My mother had to *make him some more.*"

Dad was smiling that big smile of his. Mom just looked blank and shook her head. "Porridge?" she said. "What does making more porridge for your brother have to do with Haig?"

"Mom had made Thomas a bowl of porridge once," Dayle said, very slowly, "And Thomas had wasted it, so she had to make him some more, she had to *do it again.*"

"Yes! Yes!" Mom's hands flew to her face. "Do it again! Of course! Of course!"

Dayle smiled a really smug smile. "We'll simply draw another picture of Haig, this time safely at home," she said, to make sure it was clear to everyone. "It's so simple it's brilliant. Don't you think it's brilliant? I'm so clever! But Crystal," she added, glaring down at me, "Crystal doesn't think it will work."

Everyone looked at me like I was some kind of fun-buster. I shifted in the armchair and sat up straight, taking a deep breath. "I think it *would* work," I said, "Except for one, tiny detail you all seem to have overlooked."

"What detail is that, dear?" Mom asked.

"There aren't any wishes left. There are no more blank pages in the drawing book."

For a moment everyone looked stunned. Then Mom, convinced I was either mistaken or else lying to save my precious last wish for the great wizard, Bloodthorn, began to interrogate me. She even tilted a lampshade to shine the light in my face.

"What did you do with them all?" she rasped. "How could you have used up four perfectly good wishes and not have anything to show for it?"

I tutted, annoyed and embarrassed that I should be questioned in this way. Determined to prove my innocence, I counted off the fingers of one hand and explained. "The first wish was for Haig, which got us into this mess in the first place. The second one was for Dayle, who insisted I turn her into a paper doll. The third was for Dad, so he could leave a cartoon haunting the castle and come home without the Chief Magician noticing he was gone. And the fourth," I said, staring fiercely at Dad, who had gone whiter than white, "Was to bring a dead frog back to life and reunite it with its family."

"Pardon me?" Mom said.

"What?" Dayle gasped.

"Ah," Dad cringed.

"Dad insisted that I use my one and only last wish to make a frog come back to life," I said.

Everyone groaned and slowly turned in their seats to cast accusing eyes at Dad. He tried to lower his head between his shoulders and disappear. "It seemed like such a good idea at the time," he whimpered.

Dayle got up and began pacing the room in agitation. She walked behind the sofa and tripped over Cuthbert, who'd grown bored with all the excitement and had gone to sleep. Dayle stumbled over towards the window and managed to squash Melina's paw into the carpet. Merlina mewed in disgust and shot from the room. Dayle kept very still after that.

"Can't we get another book?" I asked.

"No, I'm afraid we can't." Dad let his big mouth drop down to rest on his chest. "The company that made the wishing books went bankrupt in the fifteenth century."

"But we *could* have got a new book by using the last page in the old one to draw a new one," Mom said, shrivelling Dad with yet another look from her blazing green eyes.

"Are you sure, absolutely positive, have no doubt in your mind whatsoever, that you can't bring Haig back using your own magic powers, Mrs Ball?" Dayle asked.

"Don't you think I've tried?" Mom said. "Time and time

again, but he's just too far away for me to reach him with my magic, and it's very difficult to concentrate on something you can't see."

Mom sighed. Dayle tutted. Dad let his lower jaw slide down to his kneecaps.

"If only he was a bit closer," Mom said, "Then I might have been able to do something."

"Closer?" My brain suddenly went into overdrive. "What do you mean, you might have been able to do something if he was closer?"

"If you'd sent him to some deserted island in the Mediterranean instead of an uninhabited planet on the outer edges of the solar system, Crystal, I would have had no problem bringing him back."

"But if you were *nearer* to him, you *could* do something?"

"Yes," she said irritably, "If he was *nearer*, I *could* bring him back. Which bit don't you understand, Crystal? Anyway, it doesn't matter, he's not closer, so there's no point thinking about what we *could* have done if he was."

The idea was still formulating in my head, but I could see from the sparkle in Dad's eyes that he was catching on, he understood what I was thinking. Dayle, not understanding, turned away from the window and stepped on Cuthbert's ear. He barked something about clumsy humans always stepping on his ears, his paws or his tail, and plodded miserably from the room.

I stood up with a smile almost as big as my Dad's stretching across my face. "Instead of trying to bring Haig back from *here*," I said, "Why don't *we* go *there*?"

"Yes!" Dad yelled, clapping his hands together and pulling his jaw back up onto his face again. "Yes! Yes!"

"Of course," Mom breathed, "If I was there *next* to Haig, right up close where I could see him, I could use my powers to bring him back *with us*."

"Us?" Dayle said. "What do you mean, *us*?"

I grinned at her. Her eyes widened. "No," she gasped, "Not again. Please, not again."

I nodded. Dayle kind of sagged on her feet, accepting the inevitable but not liking it very much. "We're going to another planet," she mumbled, "So your Mom can use her magic to bring Haig home again. Am I right?"

"Spot on."

"Oh dear."

Dayle tried to sneak out of the room and out the back door when Mom and Dad began discussing the plan of action. "I don't want to go," she cried, when I caught up with her. "Going to Scotland was bad enough. I can't survive another magic trip. I want to go home and be a nuisance to my Mom," she wailed. "Please, Crystal, don't make me go."

I looked down at her, now on her knees, begging me with her hands together. She did look very pale, and there were dark circles under her eyes. "Are you sure you don't want to come with us?" I asked. "It might be fun to visit another planet, and Mom's a bit better with cosmic directions that earthly ones."

Dayle shook her head furiously. "I'd rather leave the space exploration to the astronauts, if it's all the same to you," she said, clambering to her feet again. "And ... and I'm sorry I got you into this mess, Crystal. Really, really sorry."

And, with that, she left. And I let her go. She didn't have to come if she didn't want to, and it wasn't all her fault. She hadn't forced me to draw Haig, I'd done it on my own.

Back in the living room, Mom had already pulled the drawing book out of my school satchel and was huddled over the blotchy, multi-coloured coffee table examining my sketch of Haig.

"Have you ever considered taking extra art lessons?" she asked me. "I think you need them."

"After this," I said, "I never want to draw anything ever again."

Mom meticulously inspected the picture. "We might need some breathing equipment. By the look of these rock formations the atmosphere isn't likely to contain much oxygen."

"What about Haig?" I gasped, horrified. "How is he able to breathe?"

"He should be fine for a little while," Mom said. "Within the boundaries of the picture he's surrounded by an oxygen bubble created from the air that was around him when he was magicked away."

I sighed with relief.

"But it won't last long," Mom added.

"Then we'd better get going before his bubble runs out."

"Provisions," she said, standing up and taking control like an army general. "We can't leave without the necessary equipment. We need oxygen and spacesuits and - "

"I'll just nip down to Strangebury's and get them for you, shall I?" I frowned. "Get real, Mom. Where on earth are we going to get equipment like that?"

She squinted her green eyes, deep in thought. Then she said, "NASA aren't running a manned space programme at the moment. We'll just use their equipment. I'd ask Elon Musk, he's a very generous chap, but he's quite busy tossing rockets into the air."

"But Mom, isn't that stealing?"

"Borrowing," Mom said firmly. "We'll just be *borrowing* it. And we'll put it all back afterwards. I'm sure they won't mind."

White sparks flew off the end of her fingertips, and suddenly there were two shiny spacesuits lying on top of Dad on the sofa.

"Get them off!" he gasped, "They're heavy."

They certainly were. I had to drag my spacesuit onto the floor and crawl into it feet first, it was too big to lift. Mom and Dad helped me to my feet and held me up as they plopped an equally hefty helmet on my head. As soon as they let go, I collapsed under the sheer weight of the equipment strapped to my back.

"It won't feel so heavy once we're on a planet with hardly any gravitation," Mom said.

"In the meantime I feel like I've *literally* got the whole world on my shoulders."

"Oh do stop complaining."

Mom had it easy. All she had to do was prop her suit up against the wall and use her magic to put herself inside. Dad was left standing in the middle of the living room, staring at two silver creatures muttering and moaning inside the helmets.

"What about me?" he whined. "Where's my suit?"

"You don't breathe oxygen, Onthe," Mom told him. "You don't breathe at all, remember? But, if you like, you can come and share my suit with me." She winked at him, and Dad stepped through the suit with a big smile and snuggled up to her.

So, there we were. Me feeling crushed as I hung heavily over the back of the sofa, Mom and Dad canoodling in the corner. We were ready for lift-off.

Mom started the countdown. "Five. Four. Three. Two. One."

The room was swallowed up by a bright white light. I closed my eyes and it was still too bright. When I opened them again, it seemed like the weight of the world had been lifted from me and I could stand up straight. I no longer felt like I was being pressed into the ground. I was practically floating.

We were on another planet.

"Where's Haig?" I turned round and round, but could only see grey rocks and my parents, still canoodling inside their spacesuit. I finally managed to tear them apart, and we all bounced effortlessly from one enormous boulder to another – it was great fun. Then we heard a noise in the distance. Several noises. They sounded like a roar, a growl, and a scream, followed by a cackle, a grunt, and another scream.

We clambered up a steep ridge and saw Haig down below in a valley, running around inside the bars of his cage trying to keep a snarling group of monsters from biting his arms off.

"Hang on, Haig!" I screamed down to him, "We're coming!" But my cries remained firmly inside my helmet and Haig didn't hear me.

We quickly bounced down the precipice, narrowly missing a jagged batch of stalagmites. The dust we stirred up with our heavy boots attracted the monsters attention. They swivelled round, saw us falling down the slope towards them like foil-wrapped meals, and decided to come over and meet us half way. Their huge bodies lumbered towards us. We slithered to a stop.

"Okay," I said, not daring to move a muscle in case I made these long-fanged beasts pounce, "What do we do now? Mom? Dad? Any suggestions? *Anyone?*"

To my amazement, Mom waddled passed me and into the throng of vicious animals without a care in the world. Dad, however, shrank down inside her spacesuit and hid underneath her armpit. The monsters growled. They roared and bared their fangs and glared hungrily at Mom.

"Right then," Mom said with great authority, clapping her hands together like a school teacher, "You've had your fun, now you can all go home."

"Says who?" snarled a green fur-ball standing at the back of the mob.

"Says *me*," Mom replied, narrowing her eyes into tiny slits and glaring back at the monster who had dared to speak.

"Says you and who's army?" it grunted back.

Mom pushed her way through the muttering creatures until she was directly level with the cheeky monster's bellybutton. She titled her head right the way back to look up at him.

"Listen here," she said, sternly wagging a finger, "When I say go home, you'd *better* go home, or else."

"Or else what?"

"Or else I'll turn you into a cheese omelette."

The other monsters licked their lips. "What's a cheese omelette?" the green monster asked.

Mom tutted. "Don't you know anything? What *do* they teach you in school these days? You're so *stupid*."

The gang of monsters all fell silent. I was rigid with fear, terrified that Mom had gone too far and was about to be gobbled up by some alien creatures I had drawn in a children's book. How could I help her if they attacked? How would I get home? How would I ever explain to anyone what had happened to my Mom?

Dad was obviously having the same thoughts, and came shooting out from under Mom's armpit to take refuge behind a big rock.

"A cheese omelette is a dish made out of scrambled eggs,"

Mom said. "A bit like this."

There was a flash and whine that slowly faded into a hum, and then there was this dinner plate lying on the dusty ground. Steam rose up off a neatly cooked omelette. There was no sign of the huge hairy green monster. The other monsters noticed this, screamed, and made a hasty retreat to the other side of the planet.

While Mom rubbed her gloved hands together and congratulated herself on a job well done, I ran up to the bars of the cage and peered inside. Haig was lying on the floor, quiet and still, with his eyes closed. For one awful moment I thought he was dead, then I saw his chest moving up and down as he breathed. He'd fainted, or collapsed, or was taking a quick nap.

He looked different. Not at all like the Haig I had known and hated. The spiky blond stubble on his head had grown almost down to his shoulders, and the protruding bulge of his big belly had gone. His clothes hung off him like rags.

"Haig?" I whispered. "Haig?"

He opened his eyes and stared up at me. "I want to go home," he said in a tiny voice.

"Yes, yes, we'll take you home."

He sat up, shook his head, rubbed his eyes, and looked at me again. "Glassy?" he said. "Glassy, is that you, is that really you?"

"I've come to rescue you, Haig." A cough came from behind me as Mom waited to be given some credit. "*We've* come to rescue you," I said.

Haig immediately started to cry. It was a sad sight, the school bully reduced to tears. I felt very ashamed.

"It's okay," I told him, touching his hand as he clung to the bars of his cage. "Everything is going to be okay."

Having travelled to a distant planet and dispersed a mob of monsters, our next task was to figure out how to get Haig out of the cage. I hadn't drawn any doors.

"You've lost a lot of weight," I said to him, "Perhaps you could squeeze through the bars?"

He tried. He was thin, but not that thin.

Dad came out from behind the big rock and suggested we

try to lift the cage up as there didn't appear to be any floor underneath, just the ground. But a ghost, a frightened boy and a teenage girl is no match for a huge metal cage, even on a planet with hardly any gravitation.

Mom did nothing to help. She arranged herself elegantly on a boulder, removed her shiny space gloves and proceeded to file her long fingernails. She didn't like the idea of having to work up a sweat in order to rescue Haig, and she was also annoyed with Dad.

"You deserted me, Onthe, in the face of monstrous danger," she said. "Deserted me when I needed you the most. And I thought you loved me."

Dad rushed over to fall on his knees at her feet. "Forgive me, Masquie," he begged. "I swear I'll never let you down again."

Haig looked at me as I struggled to lift the cage on my own. "Who are they?" he asked, tilting his head towards the now smooching couple on the rock.

"They're my parents," I shrugged.

"Weird."

"Very."

While Mom and Dad made it up, Haig and I could do nothing but sit on the dusty ground on either side of the metal bars and talk. It felt strange to be idly passing the time of day with a bully who had often threatened me with death. It was hard to believe it was the same boy. Even his voice sounded different; softer, deeper, more grown-up.

"So it was you and Dayle who sent me here," he said, after I'd confessed to everything, because honesty is always the best policy.

"Yes. I'm sorry. Are you very angry?"

"I was at first," he admitted. "But I've had plenty of time to think since then. I deserved it. I've been a real pain, haven't I?"

"Well ... just a bit."

We laughed, actually laughed together, the school bully and I. Then Haig slid his hand through the bars and held my gloved one gently. I was so surprised by this that I didn't even try to pull away.

"If I ever get out of here," he said, "I promise I'll never do another nasty thing to anyone ever again. I swear."

I was about to say I believed him and gaze deep into his blue eyes, when Mom bounced over and dropped a heavy bag of tools in my lap.

"Try using some of these," she said. "You might be able to get him out of there. Then again, you might not."

We tried sawing through the bars with a hacksaw, melting them with a blowtorch, hacking at them with an axe, and even taped a single stick of dynamite to one and detonated it. All to not avail. The cage holding Haig inside remained firmly intact.

"What kind of metal did you use to make these bars?" Mom asked.

"I don't know," I sobbed, frantically rubbing away at a bar with one of Mom's nail files. "I just drew them, I didn't take a lesson in metal manufacturing first."

Haig was squatting on the floor, looking totally fed-up and depressed. "There's something you should know," he said quietly. "The air's getting pretty thin in here. I'm having difficulty breathing."

"MOM!" I screamed, "DO SOMETHING! QUICK! HE'S GOING TO DIE IF WE DON'T GET HIM OUT OF THERE SOON!"

I unscrewed my helmet, planning to give him some of my precious oxygen. The planet's atmosphere hissed into the suit and I almost passed out. Dad screwed my helmet back on, giving me detailed descriptions of the changing colour of my face as he did so.

"You're turning red. Now you're blue. Now you've gone a kind of reddy-purple with a grey tinge around the eyes."

"Oh dear," Mom said, suddenly laughing and putting her hands up to her embarrassed face. "I've just thought of something. I'm so silly. I really am a silly old witch. Move aside, Crystal."

"What for? What are you going to do?"

"I'm going to get Haig out of the cage."

I moved. Mom flashed bright sparks from the ends of her manicured fingernails, and suddenly Haig was on the outside of the bars instead of the inside.

"Why didn't you do that in the first place?" I snapped, throwing the nail file, the hacksaw, the blowtorch and the axe down on the ground.

"Because you never asked me to," Mom said. "Do you want to go home now, or do you want to stand around and sulk for a while?"

We had made it to the planet, fought off a mob of monsters and got Haig out of the cage. Now all we had to do was get home again. Then our lives could continue as normal - or as normal as mine ever got - and I would never mess around with magic drawing books ever again.

We did as Mom told us and stood in a line amongst the dusty rocks, holding hands and waiting for the sparks to start flying from Mom's fingertips. Home, I thought. We were going home. Haig looked as if he might start crying again.

We waited. Nothing happened. Mom's fingertips fizzled a bit, and spluttered, and flared like a damp sparkler, but the rocks remained around us. There was no bright light to transport us back to earth.

"Oh dear," said Mom, staring at her fingers and shaking them, "I seem to have a little problem."

"What problem is that, Mom?"

"Well, you know I transported those spacesuits all the way from America and into our living room."

"Yes."

"And you know I magicked myself inside the suit, then brought us all here, turned that big green monster into a cheese omelette and made a bag of tools materialise before getting Haig out of the cage?"

"Get to the point, Mom."

"The point is," she said, "It seems I've ... er ... run out of magic power. I'm overdrawn. Bankrupt. Empty."

"You mean - ?"

"You can't - ?"

"Get us back home," we all said in unison, horrified to the

very marrowbone of our skeletons.

Mom slowly nodded her head. We all collapsed onto a rock, groaning and sighing and crying a great deal.

We'd come to rescue Haig, only to find that we now needed rescuing ourselves.

CHAPTER NINE

We were done for. I was sure of it. And Haig didn't look too good. He was struggling to breathe, trying to stay alive with the last remnants of air surrounding him. I lifted my helmet up from time to time so he could have a quick gasp of mine, but my oxygen tanks were starting to run low. I was worried. Really worried.

Dad was standing beside Mom, arguing for the first time in three hundred years. As a ghost, the lack of oxygen didn't bother him, but he was concerned for the rest of us. I'd never seen him so angry or so frightened before.

"How could you have let this happen, Masquie?" he yelled. "Didn't you think to check your magic account before blasting us all a million miles through the solar system? Any normal person would have had the sense to do *that*."

"There wasn't time," Mom yelled back. "It's not *my* fault we're stranded here. It was a simple mistake anyone could have made, and you're not helping matters by shouting at me. I don't like being shouted at. It upsets me."

Dad paced up and down in front of us, walking through rocks, tutting and shaking his head with his hands clasped tightly behind his back. He looked like a pale version of Prince Charles, only with smaller ears.

"Couldn't you ask the bank manager for an overdraft on your account?" he asked.

Mom wiped a tear from her eye. "I could," she sniffed. "I'll post a letter to make an official request, shall I? It'll only take a few million light years for it to arrive, but we've got plenty of time, haven't we? We'll just sit and wait for him to reply."

And so they went on, Dad blaming Mom for wasting all her magic on face changes and household chores, Mom moaning that Dad was never home and it was hard to bring up a child on her own.

Haig and I sat close together, holding hands again. I didn't see any harm in holding hands since we were going to die soon anyway, and this was probably the closest I was going to get to having a boyfriend, and a pretty good-looking boyfriend at that.

I thought of all the other things I hadn't done yet, all the time I'd wasted in school instead of studying. We should have stayed in the cave in the Black Mountains where there were goblins and elves to lend a helping hand and keep me out of trouble. Then we wouldn't be marooned here, about to die. It was all my fault.

"I never liked being a bully, you know," Haig said. "It was just to get attention. Nobody wanted to be my friend."

I squeezed his fingers and tried to push my blue lips into an understanding smile. "Being nasty to everyone isn't the best way to make friends, Haig."

"I didn't know what else to do." He lowered his head and started trickling the grey dust through his fingers with his free hand. "I wanted everybody to like me and, when they didn't, I got upset."

"So you beat everybody to a pulp instead. Sounds logical."

He shrugged his huge shoulders. Even in our desperate situation I couldn't help but admire the muscles that rippled in his arms as a result of all that fighting. And his face, without that fierce scowl and puppy fat, he was … well, he was really rather handsome, and his blue eyes were lovely. Funny how I'd never noticed them before.

I turned away, hoping he couldn't read my thoughts. My heart was pounding in my chest and I wasn't sure why. And what were all those tingles running up and down my spine whenever Haig looked at me or spoke to me in his deep, husky voice?

I was just about to break out into a crimson blush when fear suddenly gripped my pounding heart. I stared wide-eyed over at

Mom and Dad and gasped, "My oxygen tank is empty!"

Mom rushed over to pull me into her arms and hug me tightly. I'd never seen her cry like that before. "My baby, my baby!" she wailed. "I wish I could do something. I'd do anything to get us back home again. I swear I'll never change my face or waste another magic spell for as long as I live, if I could just take us all back to safety."

Dad came over to comfort her as she comforted me. "Dying isn't so bad," he said, as Haig bowed his head and bravely accepted the fact that we were about to perish. "You get to float through walls and scare all the people who were nasty to you when you were alive. Although," Dad said, looking around, "I don't think there's many people to scare around here."

Following Dad's gaze as he stared at the planet around him, Mom started to howl again, even louder than before. "We're doomed! DOOMED!"

Then, above the sound of Mom's wailing and my gasping, Haig's hoarse breathing and Dad yelling for us all to be quiet and accept our fate with dignity, there came the rumble of thunder from high up in the black sky. Lightning flashed directly overhead, sending fingers of electricity into the ground. Boulders were split in half and the dusty ground was scorched.

"Oh great!" I croaked, "Just what we need, a cosmic thunderstorm."

We crawled behind a rock as another rumble of thunder and a bolt of lightning tore across the sky. We weren't sure if we were safer behind the rock than out in the open, but what did it matter, it was just a feeble attempt to stay alive for just a few minutes longer.

There was a great roar that shook all our internal organs and seemed to rattle the whole planet. It died away and suddenly, inexplicably, it stopped, all of it; the thunder and the lightning gone, just like that, as if somebody had come along, flicked a switch and turned it off.

The sky was dark and clear once more, but the atmosphere was strangely heavy with a thick, tense silence, like something was about to happen.

We stood up. We looked around. We glanced at the empty cage and saw that it had been struck by lightning and reduced to a smoky pile of melted metal. We'd got Haig out just in time. Just in time to die.

Within the clouds of smoke around the cage, a shape moved. We thought the monsters had returned to finish us off. The shape moved towards us, came closer, broke through the swirls of smoke, and then we saw it clearly. Saw *him*.

The Chief Magician. And he didn't look at all happy. He stood there in front of us, angrily tapping his foot in the dust and huffing loudly through his beard.

"So *this* is what you've been up to," he boomed, his voice as loud and as frightening as the thunder that had announced his arrival. "I *knew* you were up to some mischief. It was only a matter of time before I caught you."

Mom rushed over and threw herself down at his feet. "Oh Chiefy, save us, please save us and take us home."

The Magician scratched his shaggy beard and peered down at her with eyes that flashed red with fury.

"I'll do anything if you'll just take us home," Mom begged.

Those fearsome eyes moved across to where Haig and I stood close together, clutching at each other behind the rock. Dad was looking up at the sky and whistling a tune, trying to look invisible.

"*You!*" the magician roared at him, "What are *you* doing here? You're supposed to be haunting a castle in Scotland, aren't you?"

"It was too cold, too boring, and I missed my family," Dad said, rather bravely. "They needed me. They were in trouble. What did you expect me to do?" He puffed out his chest and threw back his shoulders, ready to face the wrath of the Big Boss. "I couldn't let them down. I *had* to help."

The Magician's eyes glowed with rage.

"Look," I said, stepping forward with Haig still clinging onto my arm, "Can't you moan and shout and scream and tell us off at home? Only we're a bit short of oxygen at the moment and your anger isn't going to do anybody any good if we're dead, is it?"

"And what would you have done if I hadn't arrived in time to help you?" he boomed.

"Well, we would have died anyway, but at least we could have done it quietly, without you tossing thunder and lightning all over the place and hollering in our faces."

"Indeed."

For long, agonising seconds the Magician kept us in suspense as he considered my words and our predicament. He paced up and down, making dust clouds swirl up around his enormous black robe. He scratched his beard and shook his head of white hair.

"Maybe he's run out of magic, too?" Haig whispered to me, as we anxiously waited to see if the great man would save us.

"Does the Queen of England ever run out of money?" I said. "He's the Chief Magician. He controls *all* the magic in *all* the world, and he's *never* short of a spell or two."

Haig looked suitably impressed beneath his blue, oxygen-deprived face.

Finally, the Chief Magician spun round to face us. We held our breaths expectantly. We had no choice really since there was no air left to breathe.

"I'll take you back," he said, and we all exhaled loudly in relief, "But only under certain conditions," he added.

If we'd had any more oxygen left we would have inhaled deeply and held our breathes again. As it was, we all stood there with our lungs empty, feeling very dizzy.

"You," he said, pointing a long gnarled finger at Dad, "You will go back to the castle and *stay* there until your haunting days are over. I won't punish you for this little escapade unless you give me cause to lose my temper again."

Dad nodded and smiled so wide his flip-top head fell back.

"You," the magician said, pointing at me, "You will return to school, study hard, and *never* dabble in things you don't understand until you're old enough."

"Yes, Chief Magician," I gasped, thinking that I was never, but *never*, going to touch another magic spell until I was at least six hundred years old, "I won't, I swear."

"And as for *you!*" he roared, turning Mom to stone with his blackest look, "You will try to be a *good* witch and not waste your magic powers on stupid things like face changes."

"Never," Mom spluttered.

"NEVER!" the magician boomed, "But just to make sure, I am, from this moment on, confiscating all your magic power until I'm convinced you'll use it more wisely in future. Do you agree?"

Somewhat reluctantly, but with her face a deep purple-colour, Mom had no choice but to nod her head in agreement. The Magician, satisfied that we were all suitably repentant, raised his long arms high in the air. Lightning streaked from his twisted fingernails, blinding us. A gale-force wind swept across the landscape, and we closed our eyes against the light and the rising waves of dust.

When we opened them again, the dust had gone, the wind had died down, and we could breathe again. We were back at our house, sucking fresh, clean air deep into our lungs.

For a while, nobody said anything. We just lay on the floor, gasping and coughing and breathing very loudly. The Magician, we noticed, was no longer with us, but we could feel him still watching us and we knew he would be watching us for a very long time.

We would have to keep our promises to behave ourselves, which would be fairly easy for everyone, except Mom. I wasn't sure if she could live without her regular dose of magic to wash the dishes and cook the meals. I don't think she even knew *how* to live without magic. I'd never had a proper, domesticated Mom before and, remembering her failed attempts to be one in the past, I wasn't sure I wanted her to be one now.

Haig was the first to struggle up off the carpet and onto his feet. "I'd better be off," he said, "My parents must be worried about me."

"What will you tell them?" I asked.

Haig thought for a moment. "I'll tell them I ran away. I'll say I caught a train to the seaside and got lost."

"Thank you," I said.

"For what?" he asked.

"For not telling the truth and getting us into trouble."

He grinned. "Do you really think anyone would believe me if I told the truth, Crystal?"

When he said my name I felt all squeamish inside. I liked the way he said it. He made it sound nice, like sparkles of warm magic off his tongue.

"I'd better get moving myself," Dad said, shattering my romantic mood as he followed Haig to the front door. "I'll work overtime at the castle until I've finished my sentence, then maybe the Chief Magician will let me come home once in a while."

Mom reached a shaky hand up to stop him leaving. He tried to hold it but couldn't, because he's a ghost. Mom, with a mischievous glint in her eye, said, "You don't have to go straight away, do you, my sweet, my love?"

She began to turn into a spirit. Dad smiled, the top of his head fell back, and Mom had to guide him up the stairs to indulge in some sloppy stuff.

Which left me all alone, in the middle of the multi-coloured living room, still in my spacesuit. It took me ages to clamber out of it, by which time Merlina and Cuthbert were doing their Close To Starvation act, rolling around on the floor and clutching their rumbling stomachs with their tongues hanging out. I fed them, then went to bed.

In the early hours of the morning I heard Dad sneak out of the house. He caught a night train back to Scotland. I don't think he could have faced another perilous journey on Mom's broomstick.

Despite all the dangers we had been through and the exhaustion that hung around my eyes in black circles, Mom insisted I went to school the next morning.

"Remember your promise to the magician?" she said. "We must all behave ourselves until we're in his good books again."

"But Mom," I groaned, "That could take decades."

"We'll be so busy being good we won't notice the passing of time." She wrapped an apron around her waist and tied her long black hair back. "Now run along, Crystal, I have work to do."

I wanted to stay and witness Mom doing battle with the vacuum cleaner, wanted to see her struggle with dirty dishes and figure out how to make the beds without breaking her nails. But she scooted me out the front door saying she was perfectly capable of cleaning the house on her own without my interference.

I called for Dayle. She was relieved to hear that Haig was safe and sound again, but she was nervous about seeing him at school.

"Stop worrying," I told her. "Haig has changed for the better. He's promised never to bully anyone ever again."

"I'll believe it when I see it," Dayle snorted. "A leopard *never* changes its spots."

But Dayle was proved wrong. True to his word, Haig's behaviour was nothing short of perfect over the weeks that followed. He helped the teachers carry their bags into class, held doors open for people, smiled all the time, said nice things, did nice things, and generally behaved like a thoroughly nice human being. The entire school went into shock.

At lunch times he began to make a habit of helping the first years with their homework in the playground. I even heard someone say that he was "one very clever dude." I felt quite proud of his achievements. Even the teachers started to say good things about him and give him top marks in class.

"Have you made any friends yet?" I asked, as I ran down the school driveway to catch him up one home time.

Haig had been so busy playing the Good Guy we'd hardly had a chance to speak two words to each other since The Great Escape. He blushed when I started walking at his side. Never in a million years would I have guessed that Haig Mullins was shy in front of girls, especially not in front of me when we'd been through so much together.

"I've made a few," he grinned, keeping his eyes on the ground. "It's much better talking to people rather than bashing their heads in."

"You want to be careful you're not voted Mr Popularity of the Year," I said.

"Don't be silly."

"No, I mean it. I've noticed a big change in you lately, and I like it. Everybody does. A girl in the third year came up to me today and asked me who that good looking boy was."

"Who was it?"

"You, you fool!"

Haig blushed again, deeper and redder than before. I wanted to reach out and hold his hand like we'd done on the planet, but I suddenly felt quite shy myself.

"Listen, Crystal," he said, thrusting his hands deep into his pockets.

"Crys," I said, "Call me Crys. It sounds more like an ordinary name. Nobody's ever called me a normal name before, and I'd like you to be the first."

"Thanks, I feel honoured."

"You should be," I giggled.

"Well, anyway." His hands were in and out of his pockets like yo-yos on elastic. He looked very agitated and awkward. "I was thinking, Crys, maybe you could ... I mean, if you didn't mind and if you wanted to ... perhaps ... "

"Just spit it out, Haig," I said, suddenly feeling very sad and miserable. "What are you trying to tell me? That you don't want to be friends with someone who has a witch for a mother and a ghost for a father, who sends you to a distant planet where you have to fight off monsters? Is that what you're trying to say?"

"No, no," he said. "It's not that."

"Then what is it" I was feeling more and more depressed. I thought he liked me. I thought he'd been too busy being Nice to talk to me lately, but maybe the real reason was he'd deliberately been avoiding me all this time. "You don't want me to be your friend, Haig, is that it?"

"No, Crys." His blue eyes tore themselves off the ground and looked up at me. "I wanted to ask you if you fancied going out with me one of the nights, sometime, perhaps, maybe?"

My cheeks burned, my heart pounded, and my stomach slithered down my legs and fell into my left foot. I didn't know what to say, what to do, and I suddenly forgot how to walk without tripping over my own feet.

"You mean, a date?" I stammered.

"Yes."

I sighed dreamily. My first date. My first proper boyfriend. And what a boyfriend!

"I'd love to, Haig," I said.

"You would?"

"Yes."

"Oh, great! Brilliant! Fantastic!" His whole face changed into a huge, beaming smile. Mine did too.

"Where were you thinking of taking me?" I asked. The youth club, maybe? Or perhaps a romantic stroll around the park hand-in-hand at sunset?

"My house," he said.

"Oh?"

"I've got this great video we could watch. *Highlights from World Cup Football.*"

"Oh," I said, straining to keep a smile on my face, "Nice."

"I'll call for you about eight o'clock tonight then, shall I?"

"I look forward to it." And just to make sure I didn't die of boredom watching a bunch of men running across a lawn with a ball, I thought I might take all my Harry Potter films along too, to help him get used to 'magic stuff'.

"You do like football, don't you?" Haig asked.

I opened my mouth to say Yes, changed my mind and decided to say No, and then Haig spotted Dayle waiting for me at the gates and wandered off.

"What did he want?" Dayle asked, as we both watched him saunter off down the road.

"He asked me out on a date," I said, still unable to believe it had really happened.

"No!" she gasped. "Honestly?"

I expected her to crack a joke, make fun of me, ask if I'd gone bonkers agreeing to go out with the school bully and didn't I have any sense after all he'd done to us. Instead, she just breathed, "You lucky thing."

We walked home for a while in silence. Then Dayle said, "You know, if I were you, Crystal, I'd tell me to get lost and walk home with Haig instead."

And, with that, she sprinted across the road to Haig, whispered something in his ear, and ran off.

Haig crossed the road, almost getting knocked over by a speeding car in his eagerness to get to me, which I thought was sweet. He fell in step beside me and slipped his hand into mine without uttering a word. We must have looked like a couple of idiots, walking up the road holding hands with big grins on our faces.

Enjoying each other's company, we took the long way home across the park and came across Maggie and B.W. fighting on the football pitch. They looked nervous when I approached with Haig, but didn't fly off, figuring that any friend of mine was a friend of theirs.

"That's B.W. and his wife, Maggie," I told Haig.

He stared at them, squinting. "Didn't one of those magpies poo on me once?" he asked.

"No, no, it definitely wasn't one of *my* magpies," I said, as Maggie cawed with laughter. "My magpies would *never* do anything like that, and I'd *never* ask them to do such a terrible thing just to save my own life."

Haig gave me a knowing look and smiled. Maggie and B.W. lost interest in us and continued arguing with each other.

"Leave my tail feathers alone," B.W. squealed.

"Stop bringing bits of junk back to the nest, then," Maggie cawed.

"Why don't you two try to be nice to one another for a change?" I said.

Maggie looked up at me and pulled the kind of face only a Magpie can pull. "Nice?" she croaked.

"Yes. Give it a go. You might actually like it."

"Nice? To *him*?" Maggie looked at B.W. B.W. looked back at Maggie. "What do you think?" she asked him, "Shall we try it?"

"I don't know, what do you think?"

"I'm not sure. It wouldn't hurt to give it a go for a while, I suppose."

"Okay."

And they wandered off with their wings draped over each other's backs, chattering politely about the weather and the sudden scarcity of earthworms in the area lately.

"You understand what they're saying?" Haig asked me, astonished. "You can actually talk to them?"

"Sure."

"You are one very unusual girl, Crys."

"Thanks. I think."

We walked on. "How is your Dad getting on at the castle?" he asked after a while.

"Not too bad. The Chief Magician is so impressed with his haunting he's letting him come home to visit us every weekend now."

"That's great. I bet your Mom is pleased."

"I'll say. I hardly see either of them for the whole weekend, they're upstairs chasing each other around the bedroom all the time. I could throw a party and they wouldn't notice."

"And how is your mother coping without her magic powers?"

I laughed. "She's not coping at all. At the moment she's in the middle of a nervous breakdown. It's not a pretty sight."

Mom hated being normal and was getting more and more hysterical every day. I couldn't remember the last time I'd eaten a decent meal, and the house looked like a bomb had gone off inside it, adding to the general multicolouredness of everything. I did all I could to help out, but Mom was a hopeless case, there was no denying it.

I told Haig all of this and he accepted the mention of magic and witches without batting an eyelid, as if it was something people discussed all the time. He was very understanding and sympathetic, which was more than Dayle was at times. It was such a relief to talk about it openly, after keeping it a secret for so long.

Haig and I made arrangements to see each other later that night and parted at the end of my road. I felt on top of the world and happy enough to fly into the sky, until I entered the cluttered, chaotic domains of my home.

Mom was slumped across the back of the sofa with a duster clutched in one hand and a can of ozone-friendly polish in the other. She was fast asleep. I gently shook her shoulder and she lifted her head with effort.

"The vacuum cleaner's run off with the microwave," she croaked, her hair hanging like rats tails around her dirty face. "And Cuthbert's refusing to speak to me because his favourite blanket turned bright pink in the washing machine."

I followed her as she shuffled down the hallway in tatty slippers and into the kitchen. In the corner of the room next to the sink the washing machine, that had never been used before and was only there for show, was happily gushing a tidal wave of soap bubbles all over the floor. Black smoke was pouring out of the cooker, and every surface was cluttered with bowls and crumpled packets and open tins.

"Argh! Your dinner!" Mom screamed, rushing to open the cooker door. Inside, a blackened blob lay burnt on a dinner plate.

"Never mind," I said, wrapping one arm around her sobbing body, "I'll just nip down to the chip shop again and get us both something to eat."

"I try so hard," she blurted. "But it's so difficult. I can't do it, Crystal! I don't know how! I wanted to cook you a proper dinner, but I *can't do it*. And look at my nails," she said, holding them up in front of her wide eyes, "They're all broken. And my hands, look at the skin on my hands, it's all wrinkled. *Wrinkled*, Crystal! I'm only seven hundred and forty-six years old and *already I have wrinkles!*"

I guided her to a chair and sat her down. "I'm not cut out to be an ordinary human," she cried, dropping her head onto the table with a loud thud. "I can't go on like this any longer. I want my magic back. I WANT MY MAGIC BACK!"

"You can't have it back, Mom. Not until the Chief Magician

says you can."

Mom grabbed hold of my hand and peered at me with bleary green eyes. "I'm fed up of my face," she breathed heavily. "I want to change it."

"You can't."

"And I want to wear nice clothes again, and not have to wash or iron or cook or - "

"Mom, remember what the Chief Magician said. You've got to be good."

"I've *got* to have my magic, Crystal! I can't live without my magic. If the Chief Magician won't give it back to me I'll get it from somewhere else."

"You don't mean … ? Not the Black market, Mom," I gasped in horror. "They only sell black magic in the Black Market. You're a white witch. You can't use black magic."

"I can," she said, suddenly smiling, her eyes glazing over as she stared off into the distance, "And I *will*. You just watch me, Crystal."

CHAPTER TEN

We were in big, big trouble. Mom had done something really bad. Her three hundredth and fifty-third wedding anniversary was coming up and Mom had decided to have a big party to celebrate. She thought it might take her mind off her nervous breakdown, but it didn't, it made her worse.

First she got completely hysterical about who to invite, because some guests didn't get on with other guests and would end up fighting or eating each other. Then she got into a state about what food to serve, because half the guests were dead and didn't eat real food, and the other half only ate raw meat. Then she agonised for *hours* about which dress to wear, what colour nail-varnish to use, and which face would look best at a party.

Then she went into the kitchen and *really* flipped out. I watched her try three times to make a special anniversary cake, and three times the charred lump ended up being tossed in the bin.

"Don't worry about it, Mom," I said, as she sat and bit the stubs of her nails over the charcoal remains. "We can *buy* an anniversary cake."

"Buy a cake with *what*?" she snapped. "We don't have any money, Crystal. We've never had any money. We've never *needed* money because we could always rely on my magic powers to get the things we needed. Now the Chief Magician has taken that away from me and we have nothing, *nothing*! How does he expect us to survive with no magic?"

Once again she started going on about buying some magic at

the Black Market, and once again I tried to reason with her until she came to her senses.

But this time she didn't listen. Her patience had snapped. She felt such a failure because she couldn't even empty rubbish bins without tearing the plastic bag and scattering the mouldy contents all over the place. Every room in the house was filled to bursting point with junk and rubbish. Clothes went unwashed and began to smell, dishes remained piled high in the sink growing penicillin, and Merlina had gone to live next door with people who gave her regular meals. What is a witch without her lucky black cat, without her magic?

"I"VE HAD ENOUGH!" Mom screamed, pulling at her unwashed hair, "I CAN"T PUT UP WITH IT A MINUTE LONGER!"

And before I had a chance to stop her, Mom jumped out of the chair, bolted down the hallway and out of the front door, still wearing her dirty apron. When I ran out into the street to look for her there was no sign of her anywhere.

I sat in the house, worried out of my mind, and waited for her to come back. The hours ticked by slowly, but still Mom didn't return. I eventually rang Dayle in a fit of hysterics, and rang Haig in a fit of uncontrollable blubbering. Both told me to stay where I was and wait for her to come home. They were, they said, certain that my Mom would come back sooner or later. She didn't normally leave me on my own for long periods, did she?

But Mom hadn't been acting like my Mom lately. She was behaving more and more like the Wicked Witch of the West every day, scurrying around the house muttering empty spells under her breath.

The mantelpiece clock burped nine o'clock in the evening, and I was just on the verge of calling the Chief Magician to ask him to organise a search party for her when she came waltzing through the front door and into the living room wearing a big smile. I noticed the change in her immediately. Gone was the greasy hair and the dirty clothes. In their place were a brand new set of sparkly robes and a head of flowing black locks.

And she'd changed her face. It was a stranger's face hugging me and apologising for running off like that.

"Where have you been?" I demanded to know. "Oh Mom," I said, staring at the unfamiliar face, "You've bought black magic, haven't you?"

I felt like crying. Black magic wasn't allowed. Black magic wasn't reliable and had a habit of doing nasty things when you least expected it.

Black magic was *bad*.

"I only bought a little tiny bit," she said, waving her perfectly manicured fingernails in the air dismissively.

She went into the kitchen. I followed her and watched as she cleared up weeks of mess with one bright flash from her long fingers. I was scared, really scared.

"Where did you get that face from, Mom?" I asked.

"Oh, I saw it on the front of a local newspaper in the Black Market. Do you like it?"

"I like your real face better." I lowered myself slowly into a kitchen chair. My knees knocked together and all my internal organs had bunched together tightly. Mom was acting so calm and happy, and I didn't like it, I didn't like it one little bit.

"The Chief Magician is bound to find out about this," I said. "And he's going to be really mad at you for buying black magic, Mom."

"The Chief Magician is *not* going to find out," she said, "Because I'm going to be very careful and only use the magic to make a few little spells."

"Since when have you ever used magic in moderation, Mom?"

She ignored me and floated off to clean the upstairs rooms. When I went up to my room later, I discovered it had been transformed into a spanking new bedroom, complete with new units, new curtains, a new bed and new wallpaper. Mom wasn't able to control herself. She'd already gone overboard with her black magic and the Chief Magician was sure to find out sooner or later. Heaven help us when he did.

Things got a lot worse after that. Much worse. Mom made a

huge wad of money appear in her handbag the next day, and went out shopping to buy food for the anniversary party. I went along to keep an eye on her and to try and keep her out of trouble.

In the supermarket, the check-out girl kept giving Mom funny looks as she pushed our groceries down the conveyor belt. As we were leaving, a police car skidded to a halt outside the exit doors and two policemen jumped out. They arrested my Mom, telling her she'd been recognised as a notorious shoplifter that operated in the area. Her picture had been splattered across the front of every local newspaper.

I tried to explain to them that it wasn't my Mom they were after, that she wasn't wearing her real face, that it was simply a case of mistaken identity, but the policemen refused to listen. They took my Mom away and locked her up.

I caught a taxi, crying and wondering what I could do, what could possibly happen next. When I got home I found Mom already there.

"How did you escape?" I asked, stunned to find her sitting calmly in the blotchy, multi-coloured sofa reading a magazine.

"How do you think?" she grinned.

"Magic?"

"Of course. I vanished from their grubby police car and into thin air. But don't worry, Crystal," she said, as I sat down beside her and started to worry, "I'm changing my face just as soon as I can find a suitable photograph to copy. Do you like Jennifer Lawrence, or perhaps Charlize Theron, I've always quite admired her?"

For days after police cars zoomed around our town looking for the elusive shoplifter. I continued going to school, but all the time I was desperately concerned about what Mom was up to at home. It could only be a matter of time before the Chief Magician found out.

And Mom seemed determined that he should.

"I've invited Chiefy to our anniversary party on Saturday," she said, inspecting her new Margot Robbie face in the bathroom mirror one morning.

"You've done WHAT?"

"I've invited Chiefy to the party."

"ARE YOU COMPLETELY MAD?" I cried, jumping up and down and feeling all my blood vessels swelling to bursting point in my head. "YOU'RE USING BLACK MAGIC IN THIS HOUSE AND YOU'VE INVITED THE CHIEF MAGICIAN ROUND TO DISCOVER IT FOR HIMSELF?"

"He won't notice."

"Mom," I pleaded, tearing her away from the mirror, "He'll notice, believe me, *he'll notice.* The house looks perfect, for a start."

"There you are then. He'll be impressed."

"He'll *be* suspicious. It's *too* perfect, Mom. He knows you're a useless housewife. You've never done an honest day's work in your life, and he's not going to believe you've suddenly changed."

"He's an old man," Mom argued. "He's short of a few million brain cells. He won't suspect a thing, Crystal. Trust me."

"You think he won't notice that our house looks like a show home? A blotchy, multi-coloured home," I said, glancing at the still buckled walls, "But a show home all the same."

Mom tutted and patted me on the head like a dog. "You worry too much, Crystal," she said. "Everything will be fine, just fine. You'll see."

But it wasn't fine. Far from it. Two days before the party, Mom's black magic ran out. When she said she wasn't very impressed with its performance and wouldn't be buying any more, I heaved a huge sigh of relief and prayed for normality to return. Mom rushed out and robbed a magic bank instead.

Not only did we have police cars speeding along the streets searching for a shoplifter, but we also had Goblin Inspectors combing the area looking for clues that would lead to the apprehension of a bank robber. It was a nightmare.

I lay in bed at night, unable to sleep. When I did drift off into a fitful doze I dreamt about the Chief Magician finding out and sending my Dad off to Siberia. We would never see him again. My Mom would be sent to the Wayward Witches Ward in Wisconsin,

Arizona, and I'd be left an orphan, fostered out to fairy homes all over the spirit world.

Everything was such a mess and I only had myself to blame. If I hadn't found the book I wouldn't have sent Haig to another planet, the Chief Magician wouldn't have punished Mom by taking all her magic away, and *none* of this would have happened.

Finally, despite the growing presence of police and goblins around our house, the big day arrived. I wasn't sure what to get Mom and Dad for their three hundredth and fifty-third wedding anniversary, so I made a velvet dust cover for Mom's wand - she doesn't use it very much and it gets pretty mucky under the bed she never sleeps on. I bought a wicker basket for Dad so he would have something to carry his brains around in when they fell out.

Dad came home early that morning, having received special leave from the Chief Magician for the day. Mom didn't perform any magic spells whilst Dad was around, and he didn't suspect a thing. He toured our spotless house and kept praising Mom for her efforts, saying what a good wife and mother she'd turned out to be.

I could have screamed. I desperately wanted to tell him - to tell *someone* - that my Mom had bought black magic, was a suspected shop lifter and had robbed a magic bank, but I couldn't. They looked so happy together and I didn't want to spoil their big day.

The party began in the middle of the afternoon. Mom made me wear a frilly pink dress she'd magicked up for me, and I greeted our motley collection of relatives feeling like a giant candyfloss.

Uncle Dracula came, of course, and Auntie and Uncle Frankenstein. Grandma Baker couldn't make it, she sent a message to say she was too busy preparing a special batch of love potion for Harry and Meghan. She sent Cousin Werewolf along instead. He stood by the buffet table and wolfed down all the food.

Auntie Twinkle came, bursting through the front door and flying straight towards me for a massive hug. I was really pleased to see her. Of all my nine hundred and seventy five aunties, Auntie Twinkle is my favourite because she spoils me rotten and lives in a magic cottage in the middle of a council estate - it looks tiny on the outside, but inside it's as big as a manor house.

All of Dad's ghostly mates turned up from the castle - except Janine, who Mom 'forgot' to invite. Our old neighbours from the Black Mountains came along too, as did every gremlin and goblin, fairy and leprechaun Mom had ever met. It was some party. A loony monster rave party. The house was *packed*.

Dayle and Haig came round to give me moral support, and boy, did I need it. I thought Haig was very brave to mingle amongst them all, chatting and fetching the drinks, although I did notice him shudder a bit when Uncle Dracula got too close to his neck.

Dayle stood in the corner of the room, wedged tightly between a sideboard and a lampstand. Whenever a gremlin or a goblin or some unidentified hairy thing walked passed her, she scooted them away with a breadstick. I could tell she wasn't enjoying herself very much.

Then the big moment arrived. The Chief Magician burst through the front door and breezed into the living room with a roar and a swirl and a flash of coloured lights. He likes big, dramatic entrances. I scoured his face for any sign of immediate suspicion, but couldn't actually see his face behind the newly washed can't-do-a-thing-with-it beard. After five minutes watching him and waiting for the worst, I was a nervous wreck, and there were hours to go yet.

The Chief Magician, a plate full of eyeball hors d'oeuvres in one hand and a sparkling glass of adrenaline in the other, slowly began to notice his surroundings. "My, my," I heard him say to Mom, "You have been busy, haven't you? Everything looks so ... clean."

Mom smiled sweetly. "Why, thank you, Chiefy, darling. I've even learned to cook, too."

I huffed. What Mom actually meant was, she'd found a few new magic spells that whipped up the meals for her in half the time it took her old spells. I don't know how she managed to stay so calm and composed when he stared at her with his dark,

117

foreboding eyes. I was quaking in my shoes.

Then I spotted something that almost made me collapse into a quivering heap on the carpet. There was something milling around on the floor by the Magician's feet. I'd seen these tiny creatures scuttling around the house a lot lately, but I couldn't believe they were deliberately trying to attract the big man's attention. I knew why they were doing it, and I can't say I blamed them for trying.

Because Mom was trying to cut down on magic spells so the Chief Magician wouldn't notice the increase in cosmic vibes, she had recruited all the spiders in the area to do a spot of cleaning for her. She'd given them flies and bits of cotton thread to make webs with at first, as payment for their work. Then, when the flies ran out and she couldn't find any more cotton thread, she forced them into slave labour, making them pick up every speck of dust in the house and deposit it into a tiny sack they had strapped to their backs.

They weren't happy about the situation, and they told her they weren't happy, but Mom took no notice. When they threatened to complain 'in the strongest possible terms' to 'someone in authority', Mom had locked them all in the attic for the afternoon so they wouldn't tell anybody.

Somehow they'd escaped and now stood beneath the Chief Magician in a mass protest over their appalling working conditions. Twenty-three hundred spiders jumped up and down around his feet, waving miniature placards.

"She's holding us prisoners and making us do all the work," their tiny voices squeaked. "You have to help us, you have to help us."

I rushed over and grabbed hold of one of the magicians billowing sleeves, just as he started to bend down to scratch an itch on his leg which was really a spider prodding him with a sewing needle it had found in the attic.

"Come and have something to eat," I said, dragging him into the kitchen.

The spiders scampered off in all direction, some trying to

follow the magician and keep up the protest, others trying to avoid the plodding of huge feet all around them. I asked Dayle to sweep them up with a dustpan and brush and dump them outside in the garden. She almost fainted but, when I promised her a brand new car as soon as we were both eighteen, she bravely got to work.

In the kitchen the Chief Magician questioned me about school, about Mom, and told me how well Dad was doing with his haunting. He said he was pleased with the way we were all behaving ourselves, and would be making a special announcement to us later on that evening. He was very charming and sweet when he wasn't shouting. I found I quite liked him, though I was sure he wouldn't be so sweet and charming if he found out about Mom and what she'd done.

While we were talking, the cooker door swung open and stuck out a shelf. On it was a bejewelled box full of magic that spluttered and glowed like fireworks. I hastily slammed the door shut with my foot, stammered, gasped, hummed a bit, and searched my brains for something innocent to say that would explain why I was leaning against the cooker fighting to keep the door shut.

"The sausage rolls aren't quite ready yet," I said.

The Chief Magician smiled a strange smile, and wandered back into the living room, just as the fridge ejected a box of spare magic from the freezer compartment. Magic doesn't like to be too hot *or* too cold.

The party progressed. Someone played a Monster Mash record on the stereo system, and my greedy cousin scoffed down three huge bowls bowl of Monster Munch crisps. Dad tried to do a bit of Rock 'n' Roll with a long-lost niece from the nether-world. She twirled like a spinning top in the middle of the room and expected Dad to catch hold of her hand but, because he's a ghost, he couldn't, and the niece crashed into the sideboard, lost three teeth and one of her glass eyeballs.

While all the guests were crawling around on the floor trying to find the missing eyeball, there was a heavy pounding on the front door. I tripped over Uncle Frankenstein's enormous feet, he was telling one of my dead relatives that he knew someone who could make them live again, and ran to answer it, thinking it was some late arrivals.

It wasn't.

"Does Mrs Hilda Snatchitt live here?" asked the two tall policemen who stood on our doorstep. "We have witnesses who have seen her in the vicinity and we have reason to believe she resides in the area. In this house, actually."

"N-no," I spluttered, "T-there's no-one of t-that name living h-here."

They showed me a photograph of the woman they were looking for, the woman Mom had looked like when they'd arrested her outside the supermarket, the woman who had been front page news in all the local newspapers for her shoplifting sprees.

"Do you recognise this woman?" the policeman asked.

"No, I've never seen her b-before in my l-life," I said, crossing my fingers tightly behind my back.

"Then we're sorry to have bothered you, miss." They walked off down the garden path shaking their heads.

Just as I closed the door, the Chief Magician came out of the living room and headed into the kitchen for more refreshments. He was holding Ben's head in his hands and chatting to him.

Dad floated up the stairs to the bathroom, pouring a bottle of spectral wine into his large mouth and singing, "Wherever I lay my head, that's my home." Mom followed him up, to make sure he didn't lose his brain down the toilet.

"They're after you, Mom," I hissed as she passed me at the foot of the stairs.

"Who's after me?"

"The police. They're after that shoplifter."

"Well, they won't find her here, will they?"

Dad's voice hollered from the bathroom. "My brain's stuck in the U-bend."

And, before I could say anything else to Mom, she shot off up the stairs screaming, "Don't flush, Onthe, whatever you do."

Dayle came plodding out of the living room trying to beat off a slobbering gremlin who was repeatedly asking for her telephone number.

"Cuthbert's under the sofa, whining," she told me.

"Wining and dining?"

"No, just whining."

I dragged his trembling body to the back door. When I opened it to let him out, I found a group of Goblin Inspectors standing in our garden wearing trilby hats and small white raincoats.

"We have reason to believe that a certain Mrs Masquerade Ball of the witch persuasion lives here," they all said together, snatching notebooks out of their pockets and licking the tips of their fountain pens, turning their green tongues blue. "She is wanted in connection with a recent bank robbery."

I slammed the door shut in their faces and secured it with three rusty bolts, a door chain, and an antique lock Mom had found in grandma's crypt the last time we'd popped round for a coffee. Realising there was trouble brewing, Cuthbert crawled underneath the kitchen table and began to howl. The Goblin Inspectors pounded on the back door, demanding to be let in, and Cuthbert howled even louder.

The Chief Magician came back into the kitchen, still talking to Ben's decapitated head.

"Who's that" he asked, when he saw me leaning up against the back door, singing loudly to try and block out the cries from outside.

"Gatecrashers," I said. *"MOM!"*

"Yes," the Chief Magician said, glancing around, "Where *are* your parents, Crystal? I'd like to have a word with them."

"They're upstairs - "

"Doing what?"

"Well, they're either trying to get Dad's brain out of the toilet bowl using a rubber plunger and a coat hanger, or else they're in their bedroom doing sloppy stuff."

"Ah," grunted the Chief Magician. "Do you think they'll be

long?"

I shrugged.

"I need the happy couple in order to make my announcement," he said. "I want them to hear it. It concerns them. Tell them to hurry up, would you?"

He swirled his enormous robes around and shuffled back into the living room, with Ben's head telling him all about his exploits in the war.

The cooker coughed and regurgitated the box of magic. "Do that again," I told it, "And we'll have you *disconnected*." The cooker quickly snapped its door shut.

The Goblins continued to pound on the back door like pneumatic drills. "Let us in," they hollered, "We know she's in there. You can't escape. We have the place surrounded."

"Guard that door," I told Cuthbert. "Make sure *nobody* gets in."

"Me?" he whined, shuffling further underneath the table. "Not me. I'm just a dog. Eat, sleep and chase cats, that's my job. I do *not* guard doors."

I tutted and left him whimpering under the table. Running to the foot of the stairs, I opened my mouth to scream for Mom and Dad to leave his brain or leave their sloppy stuff alone, whichever they were doing, and absently glanced through the glass in the front door. The two policemen were still outside, talking into their car radio and glancing back at the house a lot.

I screamed, I yelled and wailed and, finally, Mom came sauntering down the stairs without a care in the world. She had that look in her eyes that meant she'd been doing the sloppy stuff, not fishing for Dad's brain in the loo. Dad followed behind her, smiling so hard the top of his head kept falling back.

"The Chief Magician wants you," I gasped. "There's goblins at the back door and policemen at the front. What'll we do, Mom?"

"Nothing."

"Nothing?"

"They'll soon get fed up and go away."

"I don't think they will, Mom. They're onto you, and I'm

losing my marbles trying to deal with it all."

"Then lose them quietly, would you, Crystal? I have guests to consider."

Smiling serenely, Mom and Dad wandered into the living room. I staggered after them, ignoring the heavy pounding at the back door and pretending I didn't hear the pounding that had started at the front door. I had visions of helicopters hovering over our blotchy, multi-coloured roof, urging everyone to give themselves up through a loudspeaker. I wasn't sure how much more I could take.

The Chief Magician was too engrossed in a discussion about nuclear dynamics with Ollie the owl to make his announcement. Mom busied herself talking to relatives, catching up on all the family gossip, while Dad fetched drinks for everyone. Being a ghost he didn't bothered using the doorways from one room to the other, he simply floated through the wall into the kitchen. He forgot a tray full of glasses couldn't float through walls too and, after an almighty crash and the sound of splintering of glass, Dad emerged in the living room empty handed.

Haig had, I noticed, been cornered by a decomposed witch who quite fancied herself as a great beauty, despite the fact that she'd been dead for two hundred years. He waved his hand at me with a Help! Rescue me! look on his face, and I was about to rush over to disentangle him from the witch's bony arms when Dayle cut across my path.

"That moron over there keeps asking me if I want to see his collection of internal organs," she spat, pointing towards the offending moron who happened to be my great Uncle Wilbur. "And that one over there," she said, pointing at a lecherous vampire who was drunkenly swinging from a light bulb, "He wants to know what blood group I am."

"So you're having a good time then, Dayle?"

"No, I am not! I'm going home."

She stomped out of the living room and I glanced over at Haig, still fighting off the advances of the wrinkled witch, before chasing after her. She hurried down the hallway towards the front door and my blood froze. Launching myself into the air, I dive-bombed her legs and pushed her to the ground before she could reach out to turn the handle.

"DON'T TOUCH THAT DOOR!" I screamed, "THERE'S TWO POLICEMEN OUT THERE WHO WANT TO COME IN AND ARREST MY MOM FOR A CRIME SHE HASN'T COMMITTED."

Dayle scrambled back onto her feet, spun round on her high heels to face me, scowled a scowling scowl, and stormed off towards the back door.

"There's goblins outside that one!" I cried, and she stopped dead in her tracks.

"How am I supposed to get out of here and go home then, Crystal?"

"You don't. You can't. You'll have to stay here."

She pursed her lips angrily and stomped up the stairs, stomped along the landing into the bathroom, slammed the door shut and locked it. Thirty seconds later, I watched her run out of the bathroom chased by an alien from the planet Org who had gone to school with Dad. I watched as she raced into Mom and Dad's room, banged the door shut, then flung it open again with her face a twisted mass of fear and frustration. Behind her, two skeletons were lovingly rubbing their bones together on Mom and Dad's bed.

"My room," I said, as she stood at the top of the stairs glaring down at me with her hands in the air. "You should be safe in there, everyone's allergic to my Bloodthorn Thunderbluster Maze III poster collection."

Dayle huffed, pushed her way passed the alien, and disappeared into my bedroom.

I went back into the living room. The decomposed witch, I noticed, had pinned Haig up against a wall and was whispering into his ear. I pulled him out just as she was about to start kissing his horrified face.

"Nan!" I snapped, "You're not supposed to do that!"

Nan slunk off.

"Thanks for saving me," Haig said, "But I have to go, Crys.

Your family are just too weird for me."

"They're too weird for me," I told him. "But you can't leave the house just yet. We're under attack. You'll have to barricade yourself in my room with Dayle."

He did.

I collapsed, exhausted, onto the sofa next to a deceased knight in shining armour and a cousin who had been forcibly removed three times and still kept coming back. I picked at a bowl of nibbles on the table to keep my trembling hands occupied, and had eaten half before my cousin pointed out that they were fried ants provided for the knight because he couldn't eat proper food.

I sighed, I groaned, I glanced at the crowd of creatures all around me, and groaned again. Ollie flew across the room and knocked Uncle Frankenstein's head off. Auntie Frankenstein screwed it back on again and tightened the bolts in his neck with a spanner. A bat that had flown in through an open window was dipping its head into a line of glasses, having a wine-tasting competition with Uncle Dracula, and a town rat was having a fight with a garden mouse over a piece of cheese under the buffet table. This was, I thought, one seriously weird party.

The Chief Magician called for order at last and faced his congregation. "Ladies and gentlemen," he said. Then, looking at the odd collection of guests packed into the room, he added, "And inhuman beans."

"Beings," someone said.

"What?" said the Magician.

"There's baked beans in kitchen if you want them," Mom said.

"No, *beings*," the someone said, "Its inhuman *beings*, not beans."

The Chief Magician tutted. "Whoever or *whatever* you are, I'd like your attention please."

He already had it, although there were a couple of ghouls at the back who were noisily considering whether to go into the kitchen for some baked beans or not.

"I wish to make an important announcement," the

Magician boomed, "Concerning Onthe Ball and his lovely wife, Masquerade."

Mom and Dad moved closer to his side, smiling shyly and looking a bit nervous. Nobody knew what the special announcement was about, but I had a nasty feeling in my bones that it couldn't possibly be anything nice, not with our recent run of bad luck.

CHAPTER ELEVEN

The Chief Magician coughed loudly. He ran his fingers through his beard, got them tangled up, struggled to get them out again, then cleared his throat. I was so nervous I nearly passed out. What was he going to say? What was the special announcement concerning my Mom and Dad? Had he found out about Mom buying black magic from the Black Market and robbing a bank? Was he about to tell everyone that he was sending Dad to Siberia, Mom to the Wayward Witches Ward in Wisconsin, Arizona, and me to some orphanage for the Hopeless Children of Disgraced Parents?

"I would just like to say a few words," the Chief Magician said, announcing his announcement for the third time and making Auntie Twinkle say, "Doesn't he ramble on a lot? Just get on with it, why don't you? I've only got another four hundred and seventy-three years left to live."

The Chief Magician ignored my Auntie and said, "Right, well, unaccustomed as I am to making speeches, it gives me great pleasure to open this new coven for vegetarian witches ... Oh dear, that's not right, that was yesterday's speech, or is it the one I'm supposed to be giving tomorrow?"

Auntie yawned very loudly. The Magician tried to shrivel her with one of his darkest looks, but Auntie refused to be shrivelled and casually scraped mould off her teeth instead. The party guests grew restless. To curb the boredom they started whispering to each other as they scoffed at the bowls of dried ants lying around all over the place. A leprechaun wandered off into the kitchen to lap up the drinks Dad had spilled on the other side of the wall, whilst the two ghouls at the back of the room began discussing the merits of having boiled blood with their baked beans instead of tomato sauce.

The Magician attempted to regain their attention. "Will you all shut up and listen!" he boomed. Nobody did. Two vampires, three hairy monsters and a zombie raced towards the kitchen talking excitedly about having pickled liver and fried spiders' eggs with their beans.

"SHUT UP!" the Chief Magician roared, "I AM THE CHIEF MAGICIAN AND IF I TELL YOU TO SHUT UP AND LISTEN, YOU *WILL SHUT UP AND LISTEN!*"

"Oh, alright then."

"Thank you. Now, as some of you may already know, a few weeks ago Grande Ball displeased me greatly with her bad behaviour. As a punishment, I took away all her magic powers."

The whole room gasped. Mom blushed, Dad nodded his head in shame, making the top of his skull flap up and down because he hadn't fastened it properly.

"But," the magician continued, "I have to admit that Grande Ball has done a fine job of being an ordinary human bean."

"Being!"

"If I say bean, its bean, and if you interrupt me once more I shall have you minced and turned into beefburgers."

"Monster meat burgers," the somebody said, "I'm not a cow, you know."

"You will be if you don't shut up," snapped the Magician. "Now, since Grande Ball has proved herself to be worthy of her magic powers, I am returning them to her in the hope that she will use her spells more wisely in future."

Mom screamed and jumped up and down in delight. Then she reached out and snatched the sparkles from the tips of the Magician's fingers and pushed them into her own. "I'm a witch again!" she cried, and immediately changed her face to look like Princess Catherine.

The magician rolled his eyes. "As for Onthe Ball," he said, "He has done a remarkably good job of haunting his castle in Scotland, and has even managed to put two human be- ... two *mortals* in hospital suffering from severe shock."

All the party guests clapped loudly, drowning out the noise of the Goblin Inspectors, who had begun pounding on the back door again, and the two policemen, who heard the pounding on the back door and began pounding on the front.

I sighed, wiped my sweaty forehead, and sank into a blotchy, multi-coloured armchair by the blotchy, multi-coloured fireplace. Mom had been right all along. I had worried over nothing. The Chief Magician didn't suspect a thing. Not yet, anyway.

"In recognition of their efforts," the magician said, raising his long arms to quieten everyone down, "I am sending them off on a second honeymoon for two weeks. After all, what is a wedding anniversary without a second honeymoon?"

Everyone began cheering, except for Mom, who looked at me and frowned. "What about Crystal?" she asked anxiously. "I can't leave Crystal on her own for two weeks."

"You don't have to," said Auntie Twinkle, putting an arm around my shoulders and giving me a quick squeeze. "I'd be only too pleased to have her stay with me for two weeks. Would you like that, Crystal?"

"Oh yes," I said, grinning from ear to ear. "Can Cuthbert and Merlina come too?"

"Of course."

"And can Haig and Dayle come and visit me whenever they want?"

"Absolutely."

"And can we have parties and go to Disneyland and eat chocolate cake all day and - ?"

"Don't push it, kid," Auntie Twinkle growled, pretending to be strict in front of my Mom. But I knew that we *would* have parties and we *would* visit Disneyland *and* eat chocolate cake all day because that's what always happened when I stayed at Auntie Twinkle's.

"That's that sorted, then," said the Chief Magician. "The

honeymoon goes ahead as planned."

The guests went into raptures of delight, bouncing up and down and hugging each other with joy, and it wasn't even *their* honeymoon. Mom and Dad looked really pleased that everything had turned out so well. They held hands and stood close together, smiling happily.

"Where are you sending them to?" Uncle Dracula asked.

"The Lake District?" asked Auntie Frankenstein.

"The French Riviera is very romantic at this time of year," said the decomposed witch, quickly glancing around the room in search of Haig and, when not spotting him, launched herself onto the shining lap of the knight.

"I am sending them," the magician said dramatically, "To Venus."

Mom looked at Dad. Dad looked at Mom. The guests looked at each other, and the whole room fell so silent you could have heard a needle drop. In fact, at that very moment, the spider who had jabbed a needle into the Chief Magicians leg to attract his attention about the appalling working conditions dropped the needle on the floor, and everyone gasped, "What was that?"

"Venus?" Mom repeated. "You're sending us to Venus on a honeymoon?"

"There's no atmosphere there," Dad said, "No tourist attractions, no theme parks, nothing."

The magician grinned at them both. He lowered his head and whispered, so that no-one else could hear, "I know you've both tried very hard, but I'm not stupid, you know. I saw that box of black magic in the cooker and inside the fridge, Grande Ball. And I know it was Ben who did most of the haunting around the castle, Onthe, because he told me so."

Dad spun round to Ben. Ben knocked his own head off and kicked it under the sofa so he wouldn't have to face Dad's anger.

"So," the Chief Magician said quietly, "You'll make do with Venus as a honeymoon location, or I can easily send you to the outer regions of Siberia instead."

"No, no," Mom and Dad both said together, "Venus will be

fine, thank you very much."

The Magician straightened up. "I also have a surprise for Crystal," he said, and everyone turned to look at me. "Because she has shown a remarkable talent for making magic, Crystal will receive *personal* tuition from *me* in the great art of spell-casting, with a view to becoming my Apprentice."

"Pardon?" I gasped, unable to believe what I was hearing.

"I'm thinking of making you my Apprentice," he said again.

His Apprentice! The Chief Magician wanted *me* to become his *Apprentice*! I nearly exploded with joy. What an honour. I'd never felt so happy in my whole, entire life.

Everyone shook my hand and patted me on the back and told me what a lucky girl I was. Auntie Twinkle gave me a kiss, and Mom snapped my mouth shut and hugged me. Then she magicked up a few dozen bottles of champagne to celebrate. I felt very happy, until I remember the unwanted visitors outside the house. It was the sight of the front door and the back door standing in the hallway that reminded me of them.

"We are fed up of people trying to break our joists apart," said the green door from the back of the house.

"Yeah," agreed the red door from the front of the house, "So we've unhinged ourselves and we're calling an all-out strike until working conditions are improved."

Several hundred spiders hiding in the cupboard under the stairs cheered in support.

I stared at the doors. "If you're both standing there talking to me," I said slowly, "Who is keeping the police and the goblins out?"

The red door curled up its letterbox and smiled. From behind it stepped the two tall policemen. "We strongly suspect that you are harbouring a wanted criminal," they said.

From behind the green door came the group of Goblin Inspectors. "And we also have reason to believe that you're harbouring a wanted criminal."

I bundled them all down the hallway out of sight, screaming, "MOM! MOM! COME QUICK!"

She dawdled out of the living room with a champagne glass

in her hand. "What is it, dear?" she asked, totally ignoring the fact that I was holding eight bodies of various heights and shapes at bay with my bare hands.

"DO SOMETHING!" I hissed.

Mom thought for a moment, and then bounced a sneaky spell down the hallway and into the kitchen. There was a small explosion, a whiff of smoke, and then a woman's voice cried, "Where am I?"

"Okay, you two," Mom said, tipping her glass towards the policemen. "You'll find what you're looking for in the kitchen."

The policemen pushed passed me and scrambled into the kitchen. I heard a scuffle and a thud, a whimper and a scream, and then the two policemen marched down the hallway holding a familiar looking woman by the elbows.

"What happened?" cried the shoplifter. "One minute I'm slipping frozen turkeys into my shopping bag, and the next minute I'm here being man-handled by the long arm of the law. I never knew it was *that* long," she gasped.

They took her away, leading her through the gap in the wall where our front door used to be. Which only left the Inspector Goblins to deal with.

"No funny business now, Mrs Ball," they said, nervously stepping back as Mom stepped forward. "We know you did it. We know you robbed the bank. Now come quietly and without any fuss, and you might get away with just seven thousand years hard labour."

"The bank was *robbed*?" Mom gasped, dramatically clutching a hand to her chest. "I think you're mistaken, gentleman. I think you'll find that the magic some nasty criminal stole from your lovely bank has been returned. With interest."

The Goblin Inspectors looked at each other. One of them pulled a mobile phone out of his white raincoat pocket and rapidly punched a few numbers.

"She's right," he said, after a brief conversation, "All the magic that was stolen has been mysteriously returned to the vaults."

"Oh," said the Goblin Inspector in charge. "Ah. Right. Well, since there's been no crime, we have no criminal to arrest. Sorry to have bothered you, madam." And he tipped the rim of his trilby hat and left by the hole in the kitchen wall where our back door used to be, hastily followed by the others.

"There," said Mom, looking well pleased with herself, "That's all sorted out. I told you not to worry, didn't I, Crystal? You worry too much."

I nodded, not knowing whether to laugh or cry. Then, from inside the living room, the Chief Magician called for Mom and Dad.

"Are you ready?" he asked them.

"Ready for what?" asked Mom.

"Ready to go on your honeymoon?"

"Now?" Mom shrieked, "You want us to leave *now*, right this minute?"

"Yes. Evets's Dad is giving you a lift."

"Evets?" Mom said, "Who's Evets?"

The alien from the planet Org who had gone to school with Dad and had chased Dayle out of the bathroom earlier, raised his long skinny arm in the air. "I'm Evets," he said. "My Dad's coming to pick me up in his spaceship. We pass Venus on our way home, so I'm sure he won't mind dropping you off."

"What time is he coming?" Mom asked.

Evets glanced at his long skinny wrist and, finding no watch, he lifted the arm of a furry creature standing next to him and said, "He'll be here in about ... ten minutes."

"TEN MINUTES!"

Mom went hysterical and ran around the house throwing things into a bin liner. All the party guests followed her, each of them carrying a plastic bag and every one screaming in a wild frenzy. They raced up the stairs and disappeared into Mom's bedroom, where there was much banging and throwing open of wardrobe doors. Then Mom sprinted back across the landing, shrieking, "My shoes! Where are my shoes?"

Haig and Dayle - forced out of my bedroom in the mad search for shoes - were chased down the stairs by the bag-wielding mob and had to throw themselves into the hallway cupboard to avoid being trampled. The mob thudded into the kitchen, picking things up as they went, with Mom screaming, "My wand! I can't possibly leave without my gold, diamond-studded wand given to me by the third Tsar of Russia!"

Seven minutes later almost every single item of clothing and shoewear in the house had been tossed into bin liners and piled up like a black mountain in the middle of the living room. Because there was no room left in the living room, we all had to squeeze together like sardines in the kitchen. A real sardine poked its head around the hole in the wall where the back door used to be and muttered, "I'm not going in there, it's too crowded."

The magician cleared his throat, and Auntie Twinkle groaned, "Oh no, not another speech."

"Have a nice time," the Magician said to Mom and Dad.

Everyone stayed silent, waiting for him to say more. When he didn't, Auntie Twinkle asked, "Is that it?"

The Magician nodded, and Auntie Twinkle smiled a great big smile and said, "Let's see the happy couple off, then, shall we?"

Everybody rushed across the kitchen towards the garden. Auntie Twinkle kept a firm hold of my hand and dragged me along with them. In the ensuing scramble to get through hole in the back wall, one skeleton was smashed to pieces and had to be carried out in a Strangebury's carrier bag, Uncle Frankenstein's head fell off again, Uncle Dracula's teeth got stuck in the wall and had to be prised out with pliers, and the knight in shining armour was crushed beyond repair and had to be cut free with a can opener.

Finally, wailing and complaining, we all stood outside in the garden. Seeing no spaceship parked on the lawn, we threw our heads back to stare at the star-speckled sky, and Uncle Frankenstein's head fell off again.

"Where is it?" I asked.

"I think it rolled over here somewhere," said Uncle Frankenstein, crawling across the lawn on his hands and knees.

"Not your head, the spaceship. Where's the spaceship?"

Ninety-five faces turned to look at Evets. Evets squinted his big black eyes at the stars, then pointed at a bright light zigzagging across the sky. "I think that's him," he said.

We looked up once more. Uncle Frankenstein, who had only just put his head back on, promptly lost it again.

The bright light in the sky grew bigger as it wiggled towards us. Suddenly, an enormous spaceship crashed into the roof of our house and the roof collapsed, sending blotchy, multi-coloured tiles raining down like wedding confetti, only heavier. The spaceship backfired, slipped off the roof, and embedded itself sideways in the lawn, narrowly missing the skeleton, who was spread out on the grass trying to glue himself back together again.

"Dad!" Evets cried.

Something that was pressed up against a window like splattered green chewing gum, said, "Yes, son?"

"Can we give Mr and Mrs Ball a lift to Venus?"

The chewing gum pulled itself away from the window with a wet squelch, formed into a face that smiled a wobbly wet smile, and said, "Sure, it's on our way."

Mom went hysterical again. "My things!" she screamed, "I must have my things!"

All the party guests ran into the house to collect the plastic bin liners, while I stayed outside with Auntie Twinkle. With a nudge and a wink, she reached into her huge black robe and pulled out a chocolate bar the size of a concrete paving slab. I gleefully tucked in as Dad, Evets's Dad and Cuthbert dug the spaceship out of the lawn. It fell flat on top of the skeleton trying to glue itself back together, and it's bones stuck to the underside.

"I'm ready," Mom finally declared, when all the bin liners had been loaded on board and the sides of the spaceship saucer bulged like a bag of marbles. Dad sighed in relief, the Magician rolled his eyes, and everyone else went "Phew!"

Mom ticked off a list, then smiled. We all smiled with her. "Just one more thing," she said, and several smiles fell to the ground and went scurrying off into a hedge. Mom marched back into the house.

"What are you doing?" I hissed, tearing myself away from the slab of chocolate and following her, "Everyone's waiting, and Venus will be out of orbit soon if you don't hurry up."

"A face," she said, sitting down at the kitchen table and casually flicking through a magazine, "I *must* have a nice Going Away face."

The Magician appeared in the hole in the wall where the back door used to be. "Grande Ball!" he boomed, "You're not wasting magic, are you?"

Mom jumped up, spluttering, "No, Chiefy. Me, Chiefy? Certainly not, Chiefy!"

The Magician growled through his beard and Mom went back outside.

I was about to rejoin the farewell party when I remembered there were a couple of guests missing. Dayle and Haig were still in the cupboard under the stairs. I ran down the hallway and threw open the door. They were playing cards by torchlight and looking very fed up as they sat amongst thousands of spiders who were all sleeping on their backs with their legs in the air.

"Do you want to see my Mom and Dad blast off to Venus in a spaceship from the planet Org?" I asked them.

Haig glanced at Dayle and laughed. "A few weeks ago a question like that would have sounded a bit strange," he said, clambering out of the cupboard, "But now it seems pretty normal."

He took hold of my hand as we all trooped outside. Mom and Dad were kissing everyone goodbye. It took ages, and Evets's Dad kept looking at the watch on the wrist of the furry creature. The furry creature eventually *gave* him the watch. Evets's Dad ate it.

Haig quite enjoyed the kiss from my Mom, but Dayle went as stiff as a plank when Dad brushed his ghostly face against her cheek. Cuthbert got a pat, and Merlina, who looked completely bored with the whole thing, got a stroke. Then it was mine and Auntie Twinkle's turn.

"You will look after my darling Crystal, won't you?" Mom asked, kissing and hugging me so tight I could hardly breathe.

"Don't you worry about a thing," Auntie Twinkle told her.

"You'll take good care of her?" *Kiss, kiss, hug, hug.*

"You know I will."

"And you'll make sure she gets to school on time every day?"

"Oh Mom!" I groaned, pulling her lips away from my chocolate-covered face before they stuck there, "Do I *have* to go to school?"

"Yes, you do," she said, finally releasing me from her vice-like grip. "And don't forget your homework. And remember to feed Cuthbert. And behave yourself for Auntie Twinkle and - "

"Mom, stop fussing."

"Okay."

Mom gave me one last rib-crushing squeeze, then she and Dad turned to walk to the spaceship, throwing hundreds of sparkly kisses at everyone. I blew some back as they struggled into the narrow space between all the bin liners, and our kisses clashed in mid-air and exploded like firecrackers. Then Mom and Dad wriggled out of sight and the door slammed shut. I felt a bit sad to see them go, but two weeks wasn't such a long time, and I was really excited about staying with Auntie Twinkle.

The spaceship started up. It hummed and vibrated, backfired twice, and sent a whoosh of fire shooting across the garden. A fence was incinerated and, behind the smoking ashes, our neighbours stood with their eyes bulging and their mouths hanging wide. Their eyes bulged even more and their mouths hung wider as the spaceship slowly lifted up off the ground.

It went up. It came down. It trembled and shook a bit in mid-air, then fell back to earth with a heavy thud. Evets's Dad tried to get it started again but, when it wouldn't, he opened the side-panel door and stepped out.

"Does anyone have a sonic-assisted, flux-expanding capacitor valve?" he asked.

We all shook our heads, except for Aunt Twinkle, who reached deep down into her black robe and brought out an assortment of screwdrivers, sweets, an entire socket set, a tin of beans, fifteen spanners, more sweets, three car headlights, a bundle of multi-coloured wires, one hammer, a lipstick and, finally, a sonic-assisted, flux-expanding capacitor valve. "I like to keep one handy for emergencies," she said, handing it over.

After the sonic-assisted, flux-expanding capacitor valve had been fitted, we all stood back as the spaceship lifted off again. It shot sideways over the heads of our gawping neighbours, circled their apple tree twice, then bounced on top their shed, flattening it.

"Sorry!" Evets's Dad cried.

"Ouch!" cried the skeleton, who was still glued underneath.

I ducked as the spaceship shot back into our garden, tilted, then pounded into our house, shattering three windows.

"Sorry!" Evets's Dad cried again.

"*Ouch!*" screamed the skeleton.

Finally, with a high-pitched whining sound, the spaceship stabilised and began to rise higher and higher into the air. Auntie Twinkle put her arm around my shoulders and slipped me a twenty-pound lollipop. Haig squeezed my hand. Dayle fell asleep on the garden bench with Cuthbert flopped on top of her and Merlina curled up on her head.

"Goodbye, Crystal," Mom shouted, opening a window to blow more sparkly kisses and almost falling out, "I'll miss you."

"I'll miss you, too," I yelled, waving like a mad thing. "Bye, Mom. Bye, Dad. See you in two weeks."

"Have a nice time," everyone else screamed, jumping up and down and waving rags and arms and bits of decomposed bodies in the air, "Enjoy yourselves."

"Help!" cried the skeleton.

The spaceship backfired again in its struggle to get off the ground with the weight of all Mom's belongings on board, and thirty-three of our neighbours, thinking they were being shot at, fell flat on the ground and covered their heads.

Then the spaceship from the planet Org that was giving my Mom and Dad a lift to Venus for their second honeymoon hissed and spluttered, coughed, sneezed and wobbled a bit, before it suddenly flew high up into the star-speckled sky with the skeleton still glued underneath and Mom hanging precariously out the window.

"Goodbye, Crystal," she yelled, her voice fading as the spaceship got smaller and smaller, "Goodbye. Goodbye. Goodbye ... "

BOOKS BY THIS AUTHOR

Tipping Point - Deborah Aubrey

Funny, sad and captivating – the struggles of marriage, family life and work, injected with a potent cocktail of sparkling humour. You'll love it.

Pitching Up! - Deborah Aubrey

A thoroughly entertaining read with a wonderful cast of charismatic characters in caravans who romp from one dramatic catastrophe to another. Touching, captivating, and very, very funny

Pitching Up Again! - Deborah Aubrey

Sequel to the much-acclaimed and very funny Pitching Up! The Woodsman pub and campsite is under new management, with new staff and improved facilities. The old gang, plus some additional characters, return by invitation to 'check it out', and the adventures begin.

Oobe Doobie Doo - Deborah Aubrey

A Short Story - A man, a suspected panic attack, heart attack, or close encounter of the heavenly kind? You decide, in this very funny out-of-body-experience tale.

Printed in Great Britain
by Amazon

33839563R00086